I0417807

Siren's Garter

Issue One, August 2016

Featuring the novella:
NEVER MARRY THE FEMME FATALE

Miriam F. Martin

Hermit Muse Publishing
Rochester, Minnesota

Contents

NEVER MARRY THE FEMME FATALE ... Page 27
Elsie Turner wants to be married to the man of her dreams. But being a career covert spy doesn't help. Nor does it help when her life goes sideways on the day before her wedding, while standing naked on the edge of a cliff. Her fiancée, Kevin Kincaid, has no idea what he's in for when he answers a knock on the bridal suite door. Bad enough he keeps his own secrets from Elsie. Too many secrets can either destroy a relationship, or raise the heat to unbearable levels.

CREATURES OF HABIT

Tom wakes up every morning to Katie's piano music. Predictable as Sunday morning. But one day while making breakfast, he discovers something missing. And he can't put his finger on that missing something. His beautiful wife makes it a habit to please him, but Tom wonders if she's holding back a secret.

GONE TO THE DOGS

Kacy spends her afternoons staring out her front window, watching the Josh the cute neighbor guy walk his pug. But as the summer heats up, she decides to put on her bikini and do a little gardening in her front yard. Not the normal method to pick up guys, but Kacy has to do what she has to do. Josh has no choice in the matter. The night isn't over yet.

THE GLOWING SATISFACTION OF PANCAKES

Kyle wakes up early morning. Karen doesn't. On the weekend, their different schedules make activities difficult. But maybe the smell of fresh breakfast could entice Karen out of bed. At least that's his plan. But breakfast doesn't end with just pancakes. Satisfying Karen takes so much more.

AFTER HOURS ON THE FULL MOON

All sorts of men drink at the Squatter's Dive bar, and Cheryl gets to meet all of them. Being a bartender has that perk, and having a little bit of cleavage helps with the tips. But the cutest guys are never single, and the one at the end of the bar seems to be no exception. He's well dressed, handsome, and waiting for a date. Pete isn't entirely sure his date will show up. But would he go for a bartender with exotic tattoos on both arms?

THE GIRL BEHIND THE COUNTER

The Quickie Mart is Jason's first stop on his way to work, and on his way home. But not because he likes the snacks or sodas. Now if he could figure out how to talk to Miranda, the girl behind the counter, he might get lucky. Or so he thinks. When Miranda needs a ride home one night, Jason decides to push his luck. Unwinding from a long day at work has never been more fun.

Quickie

Confessionals

THE GIRL UPSTAIRS

MY DOWNSTAIRS NEIGHBOR IS HOT. Smoking, hot. Tall, dark black hair, baby smooth skin. Ryan is his name. He does the yard work for our landlord. Once a week I wake up to the smell of fresh cut grass, and I hear the *clip-clip-clip* of him trimming the bushes directly below my dinette window.

The aroma of fresh Arabian coffee mixes with the fresh grassy scent. I open the yellow lacy dinette window curtains and look out below at him. I'm wearing a lacy black bra and white Brazilian cut panties. He's got on a pair of khaki shorts and tennis shoes. I hope he can see me.

So I tap on the window. Innocently, of course. *Tap-tap.* Ryan looks up, and nearly drops the trimmers. He fumbles for a bit, makes a nice recovery by catching the trimmers in one hand, and waves at me. I wave back, an impish grin flushing my cheeks. For an awkward moment too long, we stare at each other as if for the first time. Ryan looks away first, face and neck red from the sun, and he goes back to trimming the bushes.

I get an idea.

I slip on my cutest pair of wedge sandals and my nearly see-through pink bathing robe, and I go downstairs with a full bottle of ice water.

"Hey neighbor," I say, offering him the water. "You look like you need a drink."

"I do," he says, and drinks the water in one long gulp. I take the opportunity to check out his chiseled abs, and the way sweat drips down his skin.

"More where that came from," I say. It's a struggle to avert my eyes from his beltline. I manage, for a second or two, but he's hard, and he's not exactly hiding it.

Ryan grins wolfishly, as if he knows exactly what's going on in my brain. The bulge gets bigger, fuller. I want to reach out and tap it. That's exactly what I do. He doesn't flinch, or smack my hand away.

"Maybe," I say, "you should get your ass upstairs before you embarrass me."

"Embarrass you how? Like this?" Ryan undoes his pants and whips it out, he's not even wearing boxers. His cock is bigger than most of my toys, with a fat mushroom head and a thick shaft that bends upward. The ball sack is equally huge.

I push him against the apartment building, in between the bushes. Luckily, there's a little ledge for him to sit on. I slip off my panties, let them drop to my ankles. What am I doing? Fucking this near stranger in the garden between buildings? Letting him see my trimmed bush like this?

Mine is trimmed down to a cute little landing strip. Ryan is fast to touch me, and slips a finger inside while his thumb rolls across my clit. I lean in and kiss him. Tongue action follows.

My heart races. Soon I'm working up a sweat in the sweltering heat. Ryan is hot and grimy beneath my fingers. Before I know it, I'm straddling that monster cock and grinding it with my hips.

Ryan makes cute panting noises. He's trying to be quiet, to not draw attention from anyone who happens to be passing by.

Deep down somewhere, maybe in my pussy, I know what a dumb idea this is. But I'm too busy squealing in delight as the orgasm hits.

My pussy squirts, watering his cock and balls. I squeeze a fistful of his hair and rotate his head as I kiss him hard to squelch my scream.

Ryan responds by grabbing my ass in both hands and pulling me closer.

He allows me a moment to bask. I push away first, and collect my panties from under the bush. Ryan zips up his shorts, but he's still hard.

"Come by tonight," I pat him on the crotch gently. "And I'll finish the job."

"I'll bring dinner," he says, and winks.

One last quick kiss before I head back upstairs. Ryan might have a long day of work ahead of him, but he has a long night of fucking after that.

I hope he's well rested.

WHAT HAPPENS IN THE LIBRARY

IN MY LAST SEMESTER OF COLLEGE, I was an emotional wreck. My boyfriend since freshman year dumped me for a cougar. The trip to Paris I'd been planning for a year had fallen through. And I'd been rejected from all ten PhD programs I'd applied to. Life sucked, and I wasn't sure why I even bothered anymore. Time got filled with Irish mint ice cream, intense boot camp style workouts, and late night studying at the college library.

Constant 24/7 menstrual cycle described my mood pretty well. I was a psycho bitch, with a big "fuck off asshole" sign on my forehead. I alienated my friends. My grades were slipping like sand through my fingers. And I hadn't gotten laid in more than a year. Crabby was just the beginning.

All that changed one late Thursday night, on the third floor of the library. Near finals week, they kept the library open past midnight for the book freaks like me to write our term papers. I was writing three at the same time, and they were all due next Monday. Earlier, I had worked out and hadn't bothered showering after, and smelled like I'd been trapped in a sauna with ten fat men and a stick of cool gel deodorant.

I still wore my workout clothes. A pink sports bra and green shorts, and a soft black, cotton jacket.

I had intentionally sat near the printer, so I could print off some research data on hard copy and look at it while I typed my papers. The printer roared to life right before I hit the "send" button. Great, so I'd wait in line.

Next I know, a really cute guy with long brown hair and glasses shows up to check the printer. He wore corduroy pants and a red flannel shirt with the sleeves rolled up. He's collecting the paper being spit out, shuffling it into neat piles, tapping his fingers on the machine while he waits. And I'm checking him out, despite my bad attitude.

As if a fog had lifted, and revealed what I'd been missing the whole time. I'd forgotten what it was like to check out guys. And he was checking me out, with quick sidelong glances.

Despite my worst intentions, the "fuck off asshole" sign fell down, and I dropped my guard. I smiled at the guy. Miracle of miracles, he smiled back and introduced himself as Gary. Small pleasantries ensued. Then I shove my foot in mouth.

"You gonna be much longer, Gary?" I said, right as the paper jammed in the printer. Go figure.

"Shucks," he said. "Only one more page to go." He tried to open the tray, but only made a lot of noise and fuss.

"You can't just whip it out," I said, standing up. I pushed my body into his. Gary didn't budge, I rubbed one of my boobs against his arm. I hoped he took the hint. If only I smelled better.

He stepped out of the way, goofy grin on his face and a teepee in his pants. I undid the paper jam and sat back down, staring at him. The printer kept spitting out page after page.

"Thought you said only one more."

"More like one hundred. Sorry."

"What I am supposed to do while I wait for the longest book report to print?"

"See the empty private study room? With the 'do not disturb' sign." Gary pointed to one of the private rooms twenty paces away. "It's empty."

"Let's go study!" I said, trying and failing to hide the excitment in my voice. I can hardly believe what was happened when I led him by the hand.

I slammed the door shut and pushed him against the wall, surprising him and taking his breath away. I ripped my jacket off, and he pulled my ponytail. After a minute of making out, I undid his belt and pants and was on my knees. Gary was well blessed, an inch bigger than my ex, with a nice thick arch. I swallowed him entirely, hungry for what I denied myself for too long.

Right at the edge, I looked up at him, feigning innocence with quick eye blinks. Gary pulled me from my knees by the hair, shoving me roughly on the table. He pulled my shorts and panties to my ankles, and held my legs high over my head. Helpless, I waited for him to enter.

He did, one inch at a time.

All the way in, he pumped my pussy for all I was worth, until I was creamy and gushing all over his cock. He came inside me soon after, his hot seed filling me.

We had sex near contantly the whole weekend. I don't know how I did it, but I got A's on all my papers.

After college, instead of going to grad school like I planned, I took an internship in the same city Gary lived.

A summer of fucking him was worth being turned away from my dreams.

THE UKE CLUB

I BELONG TO A UKULELE CLUB THAT MEETS every Tuesday night to jam at a local coffee shop. There's maybe fifteen of us regulars, and we've been doing this for over a year. Most of us play soprano, some like me also have baritones, and a couple oddballs will bring in alto or tenor ukes now and then. Julia is the only one to play alto every week.

We always sit next to each other on the shaggy green couch, with our soprano ukes in the cases at our feet. For an hour or two every week, I get to rub elbows with the most beautiful brunette uke player in town.

I often wondered what it'd like to rub other parts of her body. One night, I got to find out.

Julia had been particularly flirty the entire session. Slapping me on the thigh when I said something off-beat, which is often. She traded jokes with me, sat a little closer than normal, and stared at me a lot.

Truth was, we'd been flirting for a long time, but I never thought she was single.

"I broke up with my boyfriend," she told me as we packed up our ukes.

"Oh?" I said, not entirely sure how to proceed with this.

"We didn't even get rough makeup sex afterwards," she continued. "I was disappointed."

"Ouch. Maybe I can help you with that?"

"I'd like that."

"Your place or mine?" I was half joking, ready to back up if she was just teasing me.

Julia gave me her address and phone number. I drove as slow as I could, giving her as much time as possible to freshen up. But I didn't want her to worry that I had cold feet.

"I was afraid you had cold feet," she said after I entered her apartment. Her studio was a ukulele mecca. One whole wall was filled with ukes of all shapes and sizes. Another wall had photographs of her playing gigs at various places. A third wall was entirely blank except for the nails sticking out of the drywall.

"That used to have photos of my ex," Julia pointed to the blank wall.

I nodded, said appropriate things, drank tasty black coffee with her on her couch. Truth, I don't remember exactly what happened. All of it was just a lovely, euphoric blur. I knew right then that Julia was the woman of my dreams. And she was all mine.

I pulled her close in my arms, and kissed her. To my pleasure, she kissed me back. One thing led to another. I grabbed her breast. She ran her fingers through my hair. I massaged the small of her back. She unzipped my pants.

It was as if somebody turned up the thermostat to a hundred degrees. Our warm bodies tangled together, meshing as if we were one. I slipped a finger up her skirt, and plucked her clitoris like a ukulele string. Eyes closed tight, she humped my finger, moaning softly in my ear.

Fully hard and aroused beyond control, I pushed her off me. Julia stammered, uncertainty in her eyes. Uncertainty was replaced with ecstasy when I turned her around and bent her over the couch's arm.

I rammed my cock inside her, pumping her gentle at first. Only when Julia begged for more did I pick up speed, my balls slapping against her. Not jackhammer fast yet, but I found a nice andante rhythm that kept her moaning and whimpering. Julia pushed her backside against me, grinding and rotating around my cock. I spanked her on both cheeks and grabbed her hips, forcing her to be still.

And then her whole body shook and quivered as if she had convulsions. Goosebumps rose on my arms, and I gave her my everything. A fast, allegro pumping.

Julia screamed out loud. It was as if somebody poured hot water on my balls as she came, the sensation driving me insane. Her juice dripped on the carpet in fat, noisy drops, making a big puddle.

I pulled out, my cock dripping wet from her come. And then I blew my load all over her back.

I let her rest facedown on the couch while I went to the bathroom to find towels. I cleaned her back gently. Julia kissed me, thanking me over and over.

"It's not midnight yet," I said.

She only smiled, and led me to the bedroom.

Months later, we still jam with the uke club, and my photos take up the once blank wall.

GONE FISHING

ON SATURDAY, AT FOUR IN THE MORNING, I put on my blue swim trunks to go fishing. I don't mean the fun kind of fishing that involves hooks and sinkers. There was a rather expensive flat-screen TV in the deep end of the swimming pool. Just part of the job of operating a hotel.

The minty toothpaste taste was still fresh in my mouth and mixed with black coffee. I barely felt awake yet, maybe because I'd been up all night auditing. But I wasn't the only one at the pool.

A buxom black haired lady in a tiny green bikini sat in one of the white lounge chairs, soaking up the pred-awn night air. I had checked her in last night. She'd arrived dressed in casual clothes that left much to the imagination. She'd been flirty with me during check-in. I blinked twice to make sure it was the same lady.

"You called about the TV?" I said.

"Yeah," she said. Her name was almost certainly Rachel. I'm pretty good at remember guests' names. "It's down there."

Rachel pointed a skinny hand to the pool. Sure enough, it was down there. I hopped in and dove to the bottom, entirely unsure how I was lifting this thing out. I couldn't quite do it, and needed air.

When I rose to the surface, Rachel was standing on the edge, and I got a good view of the bottom half of her bikini. "Need help?" she said.

"Sure," I said.

She dived in, and I met her at the bottom. Between the two of us, we got the TV to surface.

"I'd like to pay for the TV," Rachel said.

"Why?" I said. "Did you throw it in?"

"How dare you accuse me of such an immature act?" she said, grinning like a child with a naughty secret. "Of course I threw it in."

"But... I'm confused." Behind my back, I crossed my fingers, hoping this ruse was a weird, though original, way of getting me into her room. Seriously, she could've just called for towels or something.

"Come back to my room," said Rachel, winking. "I'll write the check. So we don't have to take care of it at check-out."

I followed her. Either she was an axe murderer, or she wanted sexual favors. Or she was tweaked in the head. Or a combination of all three. I was soaking wet, wearing nothing but swim trunks and a goofy smile. What did I care?

Sure enough, the TV was missing from the room. As soon as the door slammed shut, I wondered what I was doing. I had never had sex with a guest. I'd fantasized about it, but I took my work seriously and wanted to maintain the good reputation my hotel had.

But Rachel cornered me with her arms around my neck, and my stomach twisted in anticipation. She was beautiful, and eager. And it'd been far too long.

I put my hands on her waist, and pulled her close. She smelled of suntan oil, and tasted like roasted coffee. The kiss lasted for just short of eternity, and then I pushed her away.

She had the look of animal lust in her eyes. My cock throbbed, fully erect and ready for play. I could've left, just told her no, maybe forget this ever happened.

My mistake was to kiss her again.

Somehow we ended on the bed, which was turned down already. Rachel got on top of me, and stripped my trunks off. Straddling my torso, she slipped off her top, and then wiggled out of the bottom.

Rachel grabbed my dick in a white-knuckle fist and pushed me into her. Her pussy walls were soaked, and not from the pool water. I grabbed both of her breasts as she rocked back and forth. Twisting her nipples with my fingers, I talked dirty to her.

"You like how I talk dirty?" I said.

"I like it better," Rachel said, "when you shut up and fuck me."

I flipped her onto her back and sank my rod into her twat. Right when I thought I was about to blow my load, I pulled out. Then I sucked on her nipples, driving her even more crazy with lust.

At four-thirty, I couldn't take anymore and I needed to go back to work. So I straddled her torso and jacked off fast and hard until I splooged all over her pretty tits. Rachel licked up the remainder of my come off my cock.

I leaned down to her ear, and said the stupidest thing I could've thought of at the moment. "Rachel, I think I love you."

"What?" She pushed me away.

"I... I love you, baby."

"Get out! Now!" Rachel pushed me off of her, clawing and scratching me.

"But, what's wrong? Wasn't it good for you?"

"My name isn't Rachel, dude! Get out!" She was screaming. She pushed me out the door butt naked, with my swim trunks in hand.

And that was the last time I ever saw Rachel—or whatever her name was—at my hotel.

THE DOOR TO DOOR PITCH

TOM IS A REALLY GOOD FRIEND, who's been with me through a lot of businesses. He's good friends with my husband Ryan, plays lead guitar really well, and damn fine looking to boot. I've joked half-seriously with the hubby that I should invite Tom over for a threesome. Ryan isn't quite on board with that yet, but has given me permission to play.

So when Ryan was out of town on business, I invited Tom over to listen to my latest business venture pitch: door to door encyclopedia sales.

He sat on my living room sofa with a cup of joe, and scratched his full head of curly black hair, and nodded.

"You don't think I can do it?" I said.

"Well," said Tom. "Does anybody buy encyclopedias anymore? From door to door salesladies?"

"From this one they will!"

"Okay. Let's hear the pitch." He was all serious now, a cute expression he does when listening. Sort of a *whatever* look, but with full eye contact.

I wore a blue pinstripe pencil skirt suit, with a pink blouse, which I had buttoned to the neck. I completed the ensemble with a cute paisley scarf. I was dressed to the nines, compared to Tom's simple t-shirt and jeans.

I gave the pitch about the great need for more information available in the home for the whole family, and the fantastic value of owning leather bound encyclopedias.

Tom sipped his coffee, listening patiently, nodding at appropriate times. After my pitch, he set the cup down. "Lose the scarf," he said.

I untied the scarf and tossed it playfully at Tom. He smirked with the corner of his mouth, and sniffed the scarf before setting it aside.

"That all?" I said, hand on my hip.

"Just a suggestion. Maybe unbutton the blouse. You know, one or two buttons."

"Eat bacon much? That's a rather piggish thing to say."

"Just try it," Tom said, winking. "You have beautiful breasts. They might help you sell more encyclopedias."

"Oh?" I undid the first button. Slow. Feeling confident, I went one more.

And then another.

Tom stood up straighter, blushing.

"You think my breasts are beautiful?" I grabbed them, pushing the girls up for him to get a better view. "How much do you think I'll sell if I go one more?"

He shifted in his seat, the bulge in his pants painfully obvious. "Try it and see."

I undid the next button, giving Tom a peek at the lacy bow in the middle of my push-up bra. He rubbed his thighs, trying to look away but failing miserably. I walked right up to him, boobs in his face, hands on his shoulders.

"Would you like to buy an encyclopedia set?" I asked, in the sexiest voice I could muster without laughing. It almost worked.

He laughed with me. "Perhaps we can make a deal."

"Oh?" I messed up his hair, running my fingers through his thick curls.

"Take off that suit, and I'll buy whatever you're selling."

I pulled my suit jacket to the elbows, and turned around. I felt a pinch on my ass, just a little friendly feel. I let it slide, and dropped my jacket on Tom's lap.

Next I pulled the pins from my hair, letting my locks roll down my shoulders. I spun around on my heels, unbuttoning even further, one button at a time. I could tell Tom was exciting, watching me, wanting to touch and holding back. The sensation of stripping for him thrilled me, pushing me onward.

At the last button I held my shirt closed, turned away from Tom, and opened my shirt wide. He moaned, and I heard him rustling about with his belt and zipper. He had his legs wide open, and I stuck my ass to his crotch and grinded him. His hard pecker stabbed me.

I wrapped my blouse around me again, turning one more time, and stripped the blouse off entirely for Tom. Then I unzipped my pencil skirt and let it drop to the floor. I straddled Tom, pressing his face against my bosom.

"You like my pitch?" I said.

"I'm just not convinced yet," he said.

"You are one tough customer." I got off him and went down on my knees. I ripped his jeans off. Next came my panties and bra. I was too excited to tease him more. I just wanted him to fill me.

And when I straddled him again, his cock practically slipped inside me of its own accord. We made out, kissing and teasing one another with our tongues. I kept getting wetter and wetter, and I rotated my hips on his member, edging him closer and closer.

When Tom bucked against me, I took the hint and rode him like he was the best ride in the carnival. Up and down, up and down. He grabbed and squeezed my boobs. I clutched at his hair, moaning ever louder as I got closer.

Tom rolled his head back, yelling he was about to lose it. I pulled him out of me, and stroked him until he blew his load all over his chest and stomach.

I licked up every last drop.

"So," I said between licks. "You want to buy an encyclopedia?"

"I'll take five of them," he grinned.

Never Marry the Femme Fatale

CHAPTER ONE

THE ROUGH DIRT CRUNCHED BENEATH Elsie Turner's sandals. She tossed her black, lace bra onto the small pile of clothes under the pine tree.

"Small" being the sleeveless orange sundress she wore up the climb to the top of Mendota Bluff, her panties, clutch purse, and a thigh holster for her compact Smith & Wesson pistol.

Anywhere else in the world, she would've left the holster on. But in the dog days of summer in small town, Minnesota, no assassins or arms dealers were chasing her up the bluff. Nothing ever happened in sleepy Wenakaga, the boringest town on Earth.

Elsie walked to the edge. The humidity clung to her skin like a silk wrap. Flies, bees, and pesky mosquitoes buzzed about, filling the empty air with their tiny music. Massive pine trees, older than the state of Minnesota, rose high above her head, and sheltered her from prying eyes who might be on the main dirt path fifty yards away.

A deer path led her to this place, a little sanctuary high above Wenakaga. She had discovered it as a child, and came here often to get away as a teenager.

Below, the Mississippi River cut through the canopy like a lazy blue ribbon. A barge floated down the water, blaring its horn, heading south-southeast, to Saint Louis or Memphis or perhaps to New Orleans. The massive boat fit beneath the King Avenue Bridge, which crossed over into the Wisconsin.

Wenakaga, the so-called "Peninsula City", was surrounded by water on two sides and was far too small to be called a town. The cute, early twentieth century homes looked like cardboard dollhouses from up here, stacked in neat rows around a ten block bustling downtown filled with bars, coffee shops, and the kind of cute stores one can only find in a small American town.

Scattered about the dollhouses were grassy parks with fountains and swing sets, larger apartment buildings empty of college students gone for summer, and more church spires than any town needed.

Near the shore of the river was the Kumonalaya Casino and Hotel, where her bridal suite and future husband were.

Elsie raised her arms in a V, closing her eyes to all of the people and cute houses below. Only somebody with high powered binoculars and a lot of time on his hands could spot her, high up in the bluffs, hidden in the pine trees. Maybe if she shouted.

She didn't care anyway. She had to come back to her home, treading through old family skeletons. Her old haunt called to her, high above the river and its small-town people.

Far away from the happiest day of her life. Which was supposed to be tomorrow.

This was was her "Howard Roark moment", which she hadn't done since moving away from home. Elsie never cared for the book, or the characters really. She just liked the image of the man communing with nature in the buff. The sex scene was hot too, at least the way she remembered it when first reading the book as a seventeen-year-old girl.

In plain view for everyone to see, yet hidden in the smallest corner.

Up here, on the Mendota Bluff, the wind whipped hard across her body, blowing her mid-back length black hair in her face, sweeping her problems away. The sun cut through the forest chill, warming her skin tenderly. Elsie breathed in, breathed out. So close to the edge, if the wind blew wrong or too roughly, she'd fall off.

Almost perfect.

She was above her problems, which shouldn't have been problems at all. At least, according to her mother.

She let her arms fall back to her sides. Rubbing her fingers on the diamond ring on her left hand, Elsie knew she'd have to face the music soon and get on with the damned ceremony.

The concept of marriage appealed to her. The reality was something else. Something Elsie wasn't comfortable with.

Was it Kevin? Did she still love him like she thought she did?

He was still the same man. Tall, close cropped blond haired with thick brows, clean shaved most of the time, with green eyes that shined in the sunlight. Kevin was a good man.

Too good for Elsie. She'd done terrible things.

No, Kevin hadn't changed since she'd met him that one fateful night in New York City.

Elsie had changed.

And he'd been the catalyst for her growth. She was a new woman because of him, and she'd be forever grateful.

When he'd gone down on one knee, diamond ring in one hand, her bare left hand in the other, the Eiffel Tower on the other side of the Seine River, what else could she have said?

No?

Fuck no. Elsie said yes, and meant it. He was her equal, and he adored her even with her many flaws.

She loved him.

But to marry the man?

Could she ever marry?

Elsie half wished an arms dealer would find her, in her sanctuary, and push her off the bluffs she loved so much. The other half knew how that would crush Kevin.

And if she called off the marriage, that would kill him as if she pushed him off a high ledge. To come back to her hometown, arrange everything with the church and the party planners, order the food and balloons, and then call it off. Yes, Kevin would die a little inside, those eyes wouldn't shine as much. And that would kill Elsie.

Soon enough, she'd have to climb back down the main dirt path, get in her blue Honda Civic, and drive to the Catholic church she grew up with. Same building on Center Street a few blocks from Wenakaga State University, same old priest.

Behind her, a twig snapped. She stiffened her back, alert now.

A camera shutter snapped.

Elsie turned.

A man stepped out of the trees, holding a red smart phone, a big grin ripped across his face. He wore a red jogging suit and white running shoes. His long blonde hair pulled back in a top-knot, loose strands of hair stuck out the sides.

In his other hand, he held her bra and panties.

"Damn it all, girl," he said. The phone's shutter sound snapped again. "Perfect!"

"Zack," Elsie said, keeping her tone calm and in control. "Give me your phone."

"Let me think about that. Um, no."

Zack Gibbs snapped another photo. He was Heidi's boyfriend, and she had been a close family friend for a long time. She was also Elsie's only choice for brides-maid, since she didn't have many real friends anymore.

A royal douche was Zack, but what to do about this loose cannon baggage? Elsie had known the man for years, and traded corporate secrets with him profes-sionally. He'd tried to get in her panties before. She'd turned him down every time.

"I'm not asking again," said Elsie.

"Or what?" said Zack. "You gonna shoot me?"

"I'd love to do just that." She looked to her pile of clothes, now diminished to just a thin sundress waded up in the dirt. The gun was missing from its holster.

Shit.

Elsie had no issue with Zack seeing her naked. Lots of men had seen her. She used her beauty to extract all kinds of lies and secrets from men. A flash of nipple and a peek under the dress loosened lips every time.

She wasn't sure if she cared about the photos he was taking. She had worse blackmail.

The asshat had taken her gun.

And that pissed her off.

"What do you want?" she said.

"I got what I wanted," said Zack. "Unless you want to give more. You know, not how I imagined things, but..."

"No. Forget it." Elsie crossed her arms, half covering herself, legs askance, trying to be intimidating.

And failing.

"Shucks," Zack slipped his phone into the jogging suit jacket pocket. "When you want your pea shooter back, meet me in room 312."

"Damn it Zack," Elsie screamed. She was so angry, steam might've been coming out her ears. "You'll pay for this!"

"No," he said. "I'd sooner get fucked in the ass. And you know how I feel about that."

He winked, turned away, and jogged down the deer path.

Elsie sighed, slipping back into her sundress.

Time to face the music.

CHAPTER TWO

ROOM 412 AT THE KUMONALAYA Casino and Hotel, the bridal suite, was dark with the curtains pulled tight, even with the blue glare of the TV. Kevin Kincaid sat on the lumpy, pure white couch he'd slept on last night, the blanket and stupidly flat pillows thrown aside, remote control in hand, bare feet propped up on the coffee table. He pushed aside his laptop with his foot, as if he could shove the problem aside.

He wore silky green boxers and a white tee-shirt. Mid-morning, and Kevin hadn't showered yet, nor shaved nor brushed his teeth. The cheap wine from last night still clung to the inside of his mouth, now dry and cotton-ball tasting.

At least he didn't have a headache. He had stopped at half a bottle. Brad, his best man and best friend, took the bottle away and retreated to his own room.

The two-room suite had a clean, new carpet smell. Yesterday, Kevin had checked in, hoping it was a dump and he'd have an excuse to cause a ruckus. He just wanted something to annoy Elsie with. Or annoy Gertrude, his presumed future mother-in-law if things worked out. A reason to give them the wrong impression.

To get out of this wedding.

Instead, the rooms were perfect. The bed, not even slept in yet, had a dozen pillows on it and fluffed to perfection. The toilet was clean and flushed nicely. The jacuzzi was big enough for three adults to sit comfortably. The mini-bar was stocked with top shelf whiskey and more Mogen David than Kevin knew what to do with.

A hangover was his latest idea. But that hadn't worked out. He wasn't one to drink much.

Kevin channel surfed, for lack of better things to do. He settled on a cooking show, where a pretty redhead was making chicken parmesan. His stomach growled, and he thought about ordering room service.

Actually, he had plenty to do.

His tuxedo still needed fitting, as did his best man's. Gertrude wanted his opinion on the cake and flowers for some reason. Father Thomas, the old priest at Saint Michael's, wanted to talk to him. Probably wanted a confession.

Kevin had more sins than he could count to get off his chest. Doing so before his wedding to the most wonderful woman he'd ever met, felt wrong. Like maybe that was something he should've done long ago.

These weren't simple confessions for a priest. The real confessions needed to be heard by his bride.

Elsie thought so much of him, and did a lot for him. He loved the way her black, curly hair fell around her strong cheekbones, the way she doted on him and teased him when he was being lazy.

The sex had been wonderful, too. Beyond wonderful, the few times they'd been together. Mind blowing, especially in Paris. She was rough and gentle, quiet and submissive at times, loud when on top.

A smile involuntarily broke out on his lips. Kevin's cock responded to the memories too. He'd been a little surprised when he woke up clean this morning. He hadn't jerked off last night, thinking he might just be with Elsie one more time, and he wanted to save himself for her. Or perhaps they'd go through with the wedding after all.

He leaned forward and opened the laptop, trying to not touch himself on the way. The hotel had free wi-fi, and it'd be no big deal to find something besides a cooking show to watch.

Right?

Instead, he opened his email. His cock instantly went limp.

Biggins, or whatever his name really was, had replied.

"MONEY" was the subject line. The message itself was simple.

Bring it.

Too many sins to explain to a well intentioned, small town priest.

Elsie would never understand. He had to get rid of Biggins, the man who never could take a hint. Or forgive.

Kevin rolled off the couch and staggered to the bathroom. The plush carpet felt warm and soft under his feet. He flipped the too bright overhead light, the fan whizzing on at the same time. The tile floor was cold as ice.

He whipped it out and pissed. Mid-stream, somebody knocked at the door.

"In a minute," he mumbled.

The knocker probably didn't hear him. Kevin didn't care. Most of the fluid in his system was water and ginger ale, sadly. He'd have made a pathetic alcoholic.

Kevin flicked the last drop off and flushed the toilet. The visitor knocked again, louder this time, quicker paced tapping. Kevin washed his hands and face and stumbled back to the living room.

Knock knock. Knock knock knock.

"Okay, okay," He peered into the sight hole. Just Brad, his best man. Kevin unchained the door and flipped the deadbolt.

"Kev, dude, come on," said Brad on the other side of the door. "Don't leave me hanging."

Kevin opened the door. Something about his best man wasn't right. He was dressed in a blue Hawaiian shirt and tan cargo shorts. His long brown hair was slicked back and tied in a ponytail. The guy was fair skinned normally, today he was pasty, as if he'd seen a ghost.

Brad was a hacker, a damn good one, but not a spy. He couldn't keep dirty laundry unless the secret was somewhere out on cyberspace. He looked about ready to burst with something.

"Hey sunshine," said Kevin. "What's wrong?"

"Dude," said Brad. "Gertrude wants to see you."

Go figure. Was it a law that your mother-in-law had to be a pain in the ass at the wrong moment? Likely, she wanted to visit the priest with him, as if she needed the excuse to go to the church.

"Can it wait?"

Brad shook his head rapidly, his eyes glancing to the left.

The blood froze in Kevin's body. The warm carpet seemed less comfortable. He shifted to the right, just enough to see the shadows across the hall.

Not much to be seen. Too many bright overhead lights. He glanced to the red floral hallway carpet.

Brad's shadow was next to another. One with an out-stretched arm.

"Whoever's out there," said Kevin. "Show yourself."

A skinny, well manicured female hand grasped Brad on the shoulder and pushed him forward. She pointed a gold plated revolver to his head.

Gertrude!

"Get in," she said. "Both of you. Jesus it's dark in here. Are you a caveman?"

She kicked the door shut with her foot. The locking mechanism clicked. The lights flicked on a second later. Gertrude pointed the gun between the two men.

Kevin opened his mouth, hands held palms out. He didn't get the opportunity to say anything.

"Can it," said his future mother-in-law. Her voice fired like a gunshot. Her hair was braided and pinned in a tight bun, the same black as Elsie's but flecked with silver. She wore a lovely purple sleeveless dress that came to her knees and six inch open-toed pumps. Over one shoulder was a Coach purse.

Brad held up a finger. "If I could intercede."

"No," said Gertrude. "You can't. I want to know one thing."

"What would that be?" said Kevin.

"What is your business with Biggins?"

Kevin's arms went numb. His penis shriveled up inside him. Something about being in his underwear in front of his fiancee's mother.

And now that not-so-sweet mother-in-law knew about Biggins, how was he going to explain it to Elsie?

CHAPTER THREE

ELSIE TURNED THE BLUE HONDA down on Summer Avenue, ten blocks from the university campus, down a street of nothing but ramblers and split-level houses. These weren't the pretty, quaint little dollhouses common in the center of Wenakaga.

The old neighborhood had been built during a boom, and the city planners must've wanted the town to feel suburban. White picket fences, old oaks taller than the houses, and neatly trimmed yards completed the everyday American neighborhood feel.

A flood of memories washed up, making the saliva in Elsie's mouth taste bitter. She squinted her eyes against the sting.

The corner where Elsie and Jane, her bestest friend at the precious age of seven, sold lemonade one summer. They made five dollars and closed shop after a week.

Dale Street, where Elsie walked to Hawthorne Elementary School. Wind, rain, snow, and sunny days. Uphill only one way.

The run-down rambler on the corner of Russet and Summer. When Elsie was young, the man who lived there was old and cranky and always alone. A real life Boo Radley, but without the heroic ending. Elsie wondered if he was still alive somewhere.

Driving though these streets while wearing only a thin sundress and no lingerie underneath felt profane. As if Elsie were disrespecting her past by being half naked.

Nothing to be done about it. And no time to be sentimental. She just needed a change of clothes before facing off with Zack.

Eighth house from the corner, on the left, was a split-level with a brick front and blue painted cedar on the sides and back. From the street, the faded sunshine yellow swing-set Elsie used to play on was visible. For whatever reason, Mother had never torn it down. Nor had she maintained it. Rust and age had corroded the metal parts, the wooden crossbeams were now haggard and rotten.

The cute rose and tulip garden in front, all the flowers perfectly spaced and at the same height, was flawlessly tended. The lawn was cut a full half inch shorter than both neighbors.

A black Lincoln Towncar was parked out front, blocking the mailbox.

The plates were from New York.

Shit on a stick.

Elsie had insisted on a small wedding, with only relatives and the closest of friends. Not like she had many of the latter. Friendship was a luxury in the corporate spy world.

Mother, surprisingly but thankfully, hadn't fought Elsie on that detail. She had dreaded telling Mom that she wanted a small church wedding, no frills, no big parties. Mom fought her on the frills, and over the parties. But less than two dozen or so invitations were sent out.

None of them to New York. The only people Elsie knew on the east coast were crooked investors and the politicians they bought. They did not count as friends. Not even worthy as close acquaintances, despite what the testosterone told the stuffed suits she seduced for information.

Elsie drove slow in front of the house. Nobody was following her. No lights were on inside the house, at least not in front. The screen door was closed shut, and the drapes were drawn tight.

She looked to the left and to the right, pretending to be a lost visitor, and drove on. Still bra-less and panty-less, and without her pistol, Elsie might as well have been naked. Now she had a decision.

Go inside to get underwear, even though she was defenseless against this stranger from New York.

Or confront Zack and get her gun now, even though she had no desire to do so without proper clothing. No telling what ideas he might have, seeing her breasts flopping around under her dress.

Elsie drove a block, turned around, and slowly came back. She sped up at the house, slammed on the brakes, and parked three houses down.

She stepped out. The street was new blacktop, and was blistering hot in the summer sun. Her skin baked. The little dress clung to her like an obsessive lover. She popped the trunk.

A sawed-off shotgun was hidden in a secret compartment and covered in blankets. Elsie wanted to take it with her. What if her mother was in danger? Too many unknowns. And carrying a firearm in small town Midwest was a good way to attract attention from the police.

No explosions this time.

And if Mom was in danger, the police were just as likely to hinder the rescue. Elsie had seen too many hostage incidents covered up by the "powers that be."

She took out the mace from her clutch purse, and tossed the bag in the trunk before slamming the lid.

Elsie strolled down the street, arranging her key-chain into a claw weapon, a key stuck out between each finger. Not like that would do much good in a fight, but it was enough to scare away a bad guy. Unless he really wanted to hurt her.

Wind blew her dress around her thighs. Walking quickly made the soft cotton material rise up her legs more.

Astute neighbors were about to get an eyeful. Elsie didn't care. She had one priority now.

At the house, she snuck around the side. To the garage.

She lifted the trashcan lid, peering inside. Sure enough, Mom still kept the key in plain sight.

With Dad gone, and her living alone now, Elsie wished Mom would take better care of herself. She knew Mom was smarter than this.

Elsie opened the door, and threw the key on the workbench.

The yellow Mustang was gone.

Where the hell was her mother?

She kicked off her sandals. Walking barefoot across the cool cement floor, Elsie wondered what the hell she was doing.

Perhaps the Towncar parked out front had nothing to do with her. Maybe the owners of that car were visiting the neighbors.

Maybe Elsie had become paranoid of everything.

But she still didn't know.

She swallowed the lump in her throat. Her heart beat faster, skin prickly and hot, all her senses in full gear.

The garage smelled like it always did. Gasoline, fresh cut grass, fertilizer.

Her eyes adjusted to the darkness now. The lawnmower was still in the same corner. So was the workbench, with tools laying out. Hammer, screwdrivers, wire cutters.

Elsie tip-toed further inside. She pressed an ear against the metal door to the house.

Voices were coming from the kitchen!

A man. He had a deep, baritone voice. Elsie couldn't make out the words.

He sounded agitated. On edge.

Good. She could use that against him.

Whoever he was.

Elsie quietly tested the doorknob. Unlocked.

She waited.

Another voice became clear. A woman's. Calm, in control, a foreign accent hidden under the surface. Russian?

The voices moved from the kitchen to the dining room. Away from the garage, to the front of the house.

Elsie twisted the knob, hoping the door didn't have a squeak.

Just ajar, Elsie peeped in. The kitchen was crystal clean. Copper pots hung over the island. No dishes were in the sink.

Muddy footprints marred the white linoleum. A man's shoes. At least size fourteen.

She opened the door all the way. Thankfully, no squeak.

She tip-toed to the island. Quick.

And set her keys on the formica counter. Elsie reached up for the biggest pot.

Stretching on her toes, she unhooked it.

And the smaller sauce pan next to it!

The crash was less than dramatic. Still much too loud. The pan bounced on the island and clanged to the floor.

In the dining room, guns clicked and got loaded.

A blond haired woman with a big rack and a .357 revolver burst into the doorway.

"Darling," she said in a Russian accent. "You must be Elsie. Call me Molly."

CHAPTER FOUR

CLUTCHING HIS HANDS IN FRONT of his genitals, Kevin's life flashed before his eyes. Kind of.

Gertrude held the gold plated revolver in both hands. Straight at his head.

Mostly he thought about how he met and fell in love with Elsie. Her sweet, easy going manner and her lovely smile. About last Valentine's Day when they'd stayed up until five in the morning rumpling the sheets off the bed.

Eyes still on him and Brad, Gertrude thumbed back the revolver's hammer. The bridal suite turned a few degrees colder, yet hotter at the same time. A shiver left goosebumps down his arms. Sweat beaded from his armpits. His body odor smelled like an over-ripe melon bursting in the hot sun, and he wished he'd taken a shower earlier.

He hadn't even noticed while watching TV.

Kevin never imagined being in this situation. In his undies, with his potentially future mother-in-law holding a gold plated gun at his head and asking a tough question.

He'd been in terrible situations, with life and death in the balance. Or with big money at stake. Never half naked. Never threatened by the mother of the woman of his dreams.

Brad was being no help at all. He stood behind Gertrude like a kicked puppy, head down, hands clasped behind his back, teetering from one foot to the other.

But this was Elsie's mother. The woman wasn't a saint, certainly not in Kevin's limited experience. She was a tough cookie when he first met her, squeezing his hand too hard, staring him down with narrow, piercing eyes.

Would she kill him in cold blood?

Was the revolver even loaded?

Palms out, Kevin stepped forward. Gertrude swallowed, narrowing her eyes. He held his ground.

And tried his best to ignore the sweat prickling on his spine.

"I owe Biggins money," he said, keeping his voice calm and even, not quite succeeding. All the practice and experience in negotiating with bad guys hadn't prepared him.

Gertrude kept a quiet poker face behind her gun, as if she had two aces in her handbag. For all he knew, she had all the cards.

"Bullshit," Gertrude said. "How do you even know Biggins?"

Well. That was complicated. Kevin opened his mouth, and decided not to spill all the beans just yet.

He had to pee badly all of sudden. Again.

Gertrude stepped forward, hot breath in his face, pressing the muzzle to his chest.

"You won't believe me," said Kevin.

"Try me," she said.

"I'm a spy."

"Government?" Her expression softened a bit. She was a beautiful woman, with a classy profile and a well trimmed figure. Like Elsie, Gertrude had a sharp nose, and a way of staring down people. Like a bird of prey, hunting small animals.

"Corporate. I work for a New York hedge-fund, stealing secrets from their competitors."

The woman's brows tightened again. "Oh? I do love a good spy story."

"It's deadly dull. I swear. I'm trying to get out of the business. Really. Before I marry your daughter."

Okay, Kevin. Keep it cool, man. Easier said than done. A lump formed in his throat, as if somebody had jammed a rock down there and his gag reflexes weren't working right.

"How are you not already dead?" said Gertrude.

Good question. What was into him? He stood up to bigger foes than Gertrude. Men who did horrible things to innocent people. But she was larger than life, even if her pumps made her a inch shorter than Kevin.

But wow, her hawk face pierced straight through him. Gertrude's eyes were steely blue, in contrast to Elsie's green.

Icy cold.

Everything else—the high cheekbones, the strong chin, the pointed brows—reminded him of Elsie. The mother and daughter were carbon copies of each other.

Kevin needed to come clean, one way or the other. With Elsie, for sure, even if it meant losing her. He couldn't live with himself any longer, not with this burning secret.

"Please," he said. "Put the gun down."

"Why?" Gertrude lowered the weapon slightly, so instead of pointing at his chest, it was angled at his privates. Her expression relaxed, and she sighed. "Do you even know Biggins's first name?"

He raised his hands in the air, shrugging. "My best sources say Mark or Martin. Others claim his name is Marvin."

She lowered the gun all the way, and released the hammer.

Brad leaned against the wall, like he was about to faint. His face was pasty pale, ghoulish. He let out a long sigh.

"Good," she said.

"Good?" Kevin relaxed, shoulders looser.

Gertrude dumped the gun in her handbag. "I'm glad you don't know. That would've implied what I was afraid of."

"Which is?"

"That you're a hit-man. Clearly I was mistaken." She straightened the purse, tugging at the strap. "I'm sorry."

"Is Elsie in danger?"

Gertrude wrinkled her nose. "Take a shower. Be quick. We need to hurry."

"You didn't answer my question."

"I don't have answers. That's why I over-reacted. Again, sorry."

"Stop apologizing and tell me what's going on."

"Biggins is after me, too." Gertrude bit her bottom lip. "And I don't owe money."

CHAPTER FIVE

MOLLY WAS A TALL WOMAN, easily had six inches on Elsie, and the blond woman wore flat patent leather loafers. She had on a tailored white pantsuit with an open-collar pink sateen blouse. Her breasts were big as ripe cantaloupes, pushed up together so they spilled out a little more than a hint. The button on her suit jacket barely held the ensemble together.

A man came into the kitchen behind Molly. He was plain looking, crew cut, big shoulders, gigantic hands wrapped around a pistol as if it were a toy. The suit he wore didn't quite fit right, the pants too baggy, the jacket sleeves too long.

He had a sexy scar on one cheek. Otherwise, he could blend into a crowd.

"What kind of Russian name is Molly?" said Elsie, hands in the air, heart pounding. She'd been held up before on the losing side of gunfights. Some things never really got easier, just blander each time. She took a deep breath, to calm her pulse and clear her head.

Molly lowered her gun, eyes flicking up and down Elsie's body. Assessed her with a cold stare and a tight curled grin. Elsie resisted the urge to cross her arms over her chest, to cover her breasts. Better to play along, play nice, and not get shot while being too cocky.

"Is this the latest American fashion?" said Molly. Her accent was thick, but more relaxed now, more bland and less Russian. The bitch sneered, upper lip raised stiff, crinkling the otherwise perfectly smooth skin. "Au natural?"

The big man with the scar shrugged, gun focused on Elsie, but pretending not to stare directly at her rack. She pegged him as a goon, but not a cold blooded one. Just a guy who liked to look, but knew how to use a gun.

"I like to surprise my house guests," Elsie shrugged.

"Surprise?" said Molly, choking on a laugh. "You're house guests? You entertain often, da?"

"I'm kind of a homebody, actually."

"Elsie, you I like." Molly lowered her gun and released the thumb trigger. "But I'm not here for you. I suggest you leave, now."

"And how do you know my name?" Elsie couldn't just leave. Not when her mother's house was broken into by Russians. Where was her mother? Apparently Molly didn't know either. Or she was bluffing, but Elsie didn't think so. Molly was too cool and too calm, in control.

"You ask entirely too many questions," said Molly.

"One of my many faults, you think?"

The blond woman opened her jacket, revealing a shiny leather shoulder holster, and put away the gun. The tight suit didn't do much to conceal the weapon. She crossed her hands in front.

"You have two options," she said.

"Only two?" said Elsie.

"You can turn and go back the way you came, and forget we ever met."

"Shucks. What's option two?"

"Nikolai and I can take you hostage until we get what we came for."

"And if I run, what stops you from putting a bullet in my back?"

"You'll just have to trust me, darling."

"And you trust me not to go to the authorities?"

Molly smiled like a reptile about to swallow a still live mouse. She stepped closer to Elsie, so that Molly's boobs were right in Elsie's face. The Russian woman had on a strong perfume that smelled of lilacs, which made Elsie want to sneeze.

Elsie resisted the urge to back away. Getting killed now wouldn't help her mother. Worse, Kevin wouldn't understand why Elsie got shot. Better to play it safe, rescue Mom, and stay in one piece to keep Kevin in the dark.

"Option two," said Elsie. She couldn't say *I'm your hostage, please handcuff me to the bathroom radiator.* Too much pride.

"Smart girl, da," said Molly. "I knew you'd make the right choice."

"Now what?" said Elsie.

"Now, you help me find what I'm looking for." Molly put her arm around Elsie's shoulders, like a big sister being affectionate, except Elsie wanted to scream inside.

"The diamonds are in the safe," she said. "Downstairs. I know the combination."

"Darling," said Molly. "I'm not here for the family jewels. I'm here for something of your mother's. A black book."

Damn it! Elsie knew Mom had gotten into something, even though she had "retired" from the spy business long ago. But she hadn't been overseas in a long time, to the best of Elsie's knowledge. What trouble had she stirred up?

Molly leaned close to Elsie, the Russian's hot breath smelled of chamomile tea and chocolate. She had lovely, thick lips and full eyelashes. Her eyes softened, full and round, less cold and more... concerned? No, more like distraught.

Elsie had bedded a woman once, when she was in her early twenties during college, and never regretted it. Sonya had been a blond, sweet as a summer's day and sassy to boot. The young woman Elsie knew so well in college had seduced her with flowers and candy. Later Elsie found out Sonya worked for MI6 and only used Elsie to get access to the university's science labs.

The experience forever changed Elsie's attitude on relationships and sex, and afterward she herself got recruited into the spy world. Only Kevin had chipped through the ice to reach Elsie's heart.

Elsie tried to untangle herself from Molly's grip, but the Russian had a strong arm. The more she struggled, the more Molly held her tight. Elsie felt helpless in the woman's arm, and her stomach tightened at the thought of how dangerous her captor must be.

"Where is my mother?" Elsie asked.

Molly pressed the tip of her index finger to Elsie's lower lip. Without turning her gaze away, she said, "Nikolai. Watch the front window for more visitors."

The big shrugged, lowering his gun, and turned away.

Elsie was alone in the kitchen with Molly.

"I will tell you about your mother," said Molly, tracing her finger down Elsie's jaw and throat. "But first you must do something for me."

"You are a sick lady."

"Da, this is true. Some might call me passionate."

"Well the answer is *nyet*," said Elsie

"But darling, you haven't heard my proposal yet." Molly drew in even closer, and brushed her lips on Elsie's.

It had been too long since the last time she'd been intimate. Elsie had sex with Kevin before they started planning their wedding, and she had convinced him to wait for it again until after. The separation would make their hearts fonder, was Elsie's reasoning.

She hadn't planned on her heart being fond for a foreign spy who might be a threat to her mother. Molly's kiss grew more passionate, deeper, with tongue. Elsie felt weak at the knees. Her stomach quivered in anticipation of what Molly had mind.

Elsie, despite her better judgment, leaned into the kiss and returned it with her tongue. She tasted the tea on Molly's breath, tongues slippery and thick with saliva. Breathing through her nose, shoulders relaxing to the other woman's touch, Elsie squirmed her hips.

This wasn't right. *She* was supposed to be the predator, not this floozy. Elsie had used the same kissing technique on countless corporate fat-cats to get them to spill their secrets. She grabbed Molly by the waist, pinched hard, and pushed her away.

The separation was breathless. And hot. The kitchen seemed like a hundred degrees with a hundred percent humidity all of a sudden. Elsie pulled her hair back, away from her face and neck, trying to cool off as fast as she could. So much of the heat came from between her legs, and she was already bare down there.

"Now, now," said Molly. "Was it really so bad?"

"Back off bitch!"

Molly smiled, the reptile grin softer and gentle. She tilted her head to one side and made one tentative step to Elsie. "We both have something the other wants."

"You have nothing I want." Elsie put venom into her voice.

Molly recoiled. The smile peeled away to reveal hurt and pain. "You want your mother. I just want us to be friends."

"Yeah? Define *friends.*"

"I meant it when I said I liked you," Molly said, regaining her composure. She held out her hands, palms out. "You remind me so much of Gertie."

Molly sighed, closing her eyes.

"How do you know her?" Elsie softened her tone. A change in approach was all. Gain the woman's trust, use that to her advantage. It's what she did for a living. Elsie stepped forward, put a hand on Molly's shoulder, and squeezed. "Please, tell me about her. My mother. You know her?"

"Da. Very well, but in another life." Molly's eyes came alive, wide and watery. She clutched Elsie by the face with both hands.

And pulled her in for another kiss.

This time quick. Just a pressing of lips.

And then pushed Elsie into the island counter. Molly grabbed Elsie's breasts, a light fingered touch followed by another slower kiss.

And then Molly went down on her knees.

Elsie grunted at the surprise attack. Her breath caught in her throat as the Russian woman lifted the hem of Elsie's sundress.

Face pressed mere inches from Elsie's pussy, Molly grinned from ear to ear, teeth white and shiny.

"My," Molly said, "you are beautiful."

The heat returned to Elsie's body. This time, she didn't know if she could stop Molly.

CHAPTER SIX

KEVIN TOOK A THREE MINUTE SHOWER and put on jeans, a white polo shirt, and a brown sports jacket. He told Brad to go back to his room, and be on call.

Then he got Gertrude into his rented Buick LaSabre, and raced off to her house.

"What's going on?" he said when he pulled out of the Kumonalaya parking lot.

"Biggins found me," Gertrude said. "And she came for a black book. Better you don't ask any more questions."

Questions got people killed. But something nagged at Kevin. What the hell was Elsie's mother into? Why was Biggins in Wenakaga? What was this mysterious black book.

At Gertrude's house, he parked across the street. Elsie's blue Honda was parked nearby, as was an ominous black Towncar.

Kevin loaded his pistol and went around the side of the house, to the service entrance. The lawn smelled of fresh cut grass and fertilizer, a very domestic odor of hard work. Gertrude tugged on his shirt.

She had her gold revolver out, ready for action, probably ready to shoot anybody who dared a lay a finger on her daughter. That made two of them, Kevin couldn't stand the thought of Elsie being tied up in a spy conspiracy.

"The side's been unlocked," Gertrude whispered, pointing to the service entrance.

"Do you always keep it locked?" said Kevin.

"Without fail."

"Any other ways in?"

"The walkout, below the deck. Come on."

"Okay, follow my lead."

But Gertrude was already in front, leading Kevin around service berry bushes and buckthorns. The yard made a steep decline around the house. Gertrude jumped over a red stone retaining wall to the downstairs patio under the blue painted deck. A wooden, disused swing-set with yellow rubber seats sat in the backyard lawn.

A set of glass sliding doors led to the basement of Gertrude's house. Kevin peeped inside while Gertrude knelt down and dug around in a tin bucket full of dirt. She produced a house key.

The tinted glass didn't allow him to see much. Looked like a gathering room, with a pool table on one side and a minibar on the other. A pink fluffy love-seat sat in between, and a big screen TV took up one wall. The walls were covered in wood paneling, giving the room a dark, dusky appearance.

Kevin nodded, and pointed to the door. Gertrude pushed the key in and slowly slid the door open without any noise.

He expected the basement to smell moldy, but it turned out to have a clean, lemon smell. The room was even more cozy than his initial outside glance. This was a place he'd like to relax, the kind of basement room where'd he'd retreat with a special lady to have a drink and shoot pool. And then make love on the sofa.

The kind of place he envisioned sharing with Elsie.

But the dream still seemed far off, especially now. Elsie deserved better. She needed somebody she could count on, and not have to stay up at night worrying if he were safe.

Noise came from upstairs. A moan. And... a giggle?

This time, Kevin held back Gertrude with an arm. He took the lead, gun in hand and ready to shoot the first bad guy to get in his way. Adrenaline pumped through his system.

He crept up the stairs one step at a time, trying to keep cool. Long training and too much practice at high stakes action had prepared him for this. Kevin was hyper-aware of every noise and scent.

Lucky, the stairs didn't creak, and were covered in soft cream colored carpet.

Upstairs, towards the front of the house, he heard somebody shifting from foot to foot. The person's shoes creaked the floor and made little tap-tapping noises.

Closer to the top of the stairs came the moaning. A slow, pleasurable sound, feminine and sultry.

And very familiar.

A womanly odor. Like a wet pussy.

Actually, exactly like a wet pussy.

Kevin stopped mid-stride, turned to Gertrude and mouthed, "What's going on?"

She shrugged and pointed her gun upstairs, mouthing back, "Just go."

Kevin didn't argue, and continued climbing the stairs. Heart rising to his throat and threatening to leap out and run away. The front half of his brain didn't allow him to process what the back half was thinking.

What kind of sick torture is going on here?

But no, that wasn't really the underlying thought rolling through his head. Kevin was scared as hell of what was upstairs, and he couldn't pinpoint a reason for his fear. His sweaty palms clenched the pistol tighter.

And he was strangely curious.

Curious to see. To get the fright over with and shed light on the weird emotions running through him.

Kevin took the last six steps two at a time, bounding like a wild animal on a blood scent. He didn't care if Gertrude couldn't climb as fast in her high heels.

He needed to know what was going on.

He ran to the source of the moaning. In the kitchen.

Pistol out in both hands, body at an angle to make him less of a target.

An island counter sat between him and...

Elsie and some blond chick kneeling in front of her.

Elsie screeched and pushed the woman away.

Kevin tried to make sense of the scene. Nothing sensical came to mind. Elsie was pulling the hem of her sundress down over her bare pussy. The blond turned to Kevin, a lovely smile on her glistening wet face. Kevin flushed, feeling hot and sweaty all over, and angry.

And oddly aroused.

A big man in a badly tailored suit burst through the other door to the kitchen, a small pistol in his meaty hands. He looked Kevin up and down, but didn't fire. Or say anything.

"Nikolai," said the blond woman, "put that away. Where are your manners, whipping it out like that in front of guests?"

He lowered the gun, slowly.

Elsie backed away against the stove range, hand pressed to her chest, face blushing.

Kevin tried to form words. Nothing seemed all that intelligent to say. What do you say when you walk in on your bride receiving oral from a sexy blond woman?

"Kevin," Elsie said, catching her breath as if she had just run a hundred yard dash. The expression on her face was pinched and blushed. Terrified and ashamed. "I... I..."

He lowered his gun, not sure what to say. Or do. His mouth moved, nothing came out at first. He was about to ask something like *what's going on here?*

But then a gold revolver came over his shoulder, in his periphery. The well manicured hand holding it thumbed back the hammer, clicking a bullet into place.

"You," said Gertrude at the blond woman. "I didn't expect you to come here personally, *Molly*."

Venom dripped in her voice as she spit out the name.

"Gertie!" said the blond, excitement tinging her voice up an octave. Molly had the worst Russian accent Kevin ever heard. "Is this how you greet me? After all these years?"

"Yes."

"But all those long nights." Her voice turned sultry, stretching out the word *long*.

"I'm confused," said Kevin.

"Shut up," said Gertrude.

"Mother!" said Elsie.

"Gertie," Molly cooed.

"Everybody!" Kevin shouted, holding his gun up as if to remind everybody he was still armed. His whole body shook with anger. He looked straight into Elsie's eyes. "What the fuck?"

His voice echoed in the tidy little kitchen, and everybody fell silent. You could hear a pin drop. Elsie stood up straighter, crossing her arms, and Kevin realized she wasn't wearing a bra. But his gaze didn't settle on her bosom for long.

He imagined steam coming out of her ears. Kevin had never seen her so angry in their year long courtship. He shared a long stare with her. They played poker later at night sometimes—with money, chips, and clothes. Both played to win. This stare was a poker stare, and Kevin felt like he'd lost count of the cards.

"You're going to explain *this* to me," Kevin said, pointing his finger at Elsie, and wove his pistol around the kitchen. "Later, when your mother isn't holding a gun over my shoulder."

And then have words with Gertrude about using him as a human shield.

Elsie blanched, mouth agape. "This is not what it looks!"

"I was worried sick about you," said Kevin. "That you might be hurt. Or worse. And I get here, and—"

And what? Kevin and Elsie had talked about their fantasies together. One of Kevin's was watching the love of his life being ravished by another woman.

Actually seeing it happen... wasn't what he dreamed about.

Elsie lowered her chin, arms still crossed, hips askance. Her *serious* stare. The pose faltered when she scrunched her shoulders up and rocked on her heels.

"There's something you don't know about me," she said.

"Yeah? What? You're suddenly a lesb... Ouch!"

Gertrude pinched him hard on the side, enough for her nails to dig through his polo shirt. "Both of you," she hissed through her teeth, "might want to save this for later."

Molly grinned ear to ear like a viper preparing to snap at a mouse. Her face was still moist from... Elsie.

"A real pleasure meeting you at last, Kevin," she said.

Kevin straightened his shoulders, finger on the trigger. He didn't want to shoot her, but the way she looked at him, like he was a piece of meat in the supermarket, made him miserably uncomfortable.

"How do you know my name?" he said.

Elsie glanced rapidly from Kevin to Molly and back to Kevin. Gertrude sighed.

"Darling," said the blond woman. "I'm Molly Biggins."

CHAPTER SEVEN

ELSIE NEVER PRETENDED TO BE THE PERFECT BRIDE. She was too far from grace to be that, and she'd told Kevin so much. But she wanted to "save herself" for the wedding night, even denying Kevin one last roll in the hay before the big day. And her last jobs were easy enough, she didn't need to pull the sex card to complete the mission. Her first night as a married woman was to be special.

And then Molly went down on her, and Elsie forgot even the pretense of chastity.

Did it count if your sex partner was the same gender?

Molly's tongue glided over her clitoris and lips, into her tunnel. Warmth spread from her hips to belly, an orgasm building slow and steady. The blond woman, despite her other faults, knew what she was doing, and did it so well. Elsie couldn't help but grind her hips on Molly's mouth.

Pussy wetter than a cat sprayed by a garden hose, Elsie had been close to coming.

The last thing she expected was Kevin to show up with a gun in his hand. To make matters worse, her mother came in behind him, the gold revolver Dad had given her cocked and ready to fire.

And why was Mom using Kevin as a human shield?

All the warm build up from being eaten out ebbed and drained down to her toes, disappearing entirely. Nerves raw and on edge, and entirely unsatisfied from being denied an orgasm, veins throbbed in Elsie's temples. Searing hot anger poured through her.

A shouting match ensued. Too many loud words, too many guns in one small room. Elsie had defused many similar situations in the past, where tempers flared and men were quick to draw weapons. She took pride in being a calm center in the storm.

This was entirely different.

This time, she felt whipped and carried away by the storm. And she had no idea why she felt that way.

Elsie wanted to kill Kevin for... some crime he didn't know he committed. Hell, even she wasn't sure why.

But then Molly said something otherwise inconspicuous, her Russian accent crumbling and turning more Midwestern. "Darling, I'm Molly Biggins."

Kevin's face blanched, as if he'd seen a train-wreck and was powerless to stop it. His hands trembled, the gun shaking, and a cold sweat broke out in his hairline. Elsie studied him carefully.

"Kevin," she said, trying her best to keep calm, but her voice shook. "Do you know this woman?"

He shook his head, but only slightly, and his eyes were plastered on Molly. Not on her breasts or legs. He was studying her face.

If she had her 9mm, Elsie would've shot Kevin herself. For once, she was thankful for Zack, though he'd never know it or even appreciate it.

"Kevin," Elsie said, sterner and with fire in her voice. She felt like a broken record. "Do you know this woman?"

Mom peeled her death stare away from Molly, and looked Elsie in the eyes. "Leave. You don't want to be here."

"What are you talking about? Mother, what've you gotten into?"

"Elsie, I love you. But you need to walk away from this."

Her mother's eyes were steel, hard and cold. Elsie knew Mom was more than she seemed. Like mother like daughter, Gertrude Turner was a spy. But what did Elsie really know about the woman? She wasn't entirely sure what organization Mom had worked for, if she still worked in the business.

And Kevin...

Elsie knew he target practiced with his best friend, Brad. But Kevin held himself like a professional. He didn't even budge out of the way for Mom, keeping his body between her and Nikolai.

She was angry for not seeing the signs earlier. The man knew how to handle a pistol, and while he wasn't entirely keeping his cool under pressure, he certainly kept his fighting posture steady. He was ready for a gunfight.

No way Kevin was just a "corporate rat" like he told her. There was a reason for all his trips to D.C. Her fiancee was a spy, he didn't need to tell her. She saw it now, in the way he carried himself and held a gun.

Was there a reason he met her in the first place? For his odd behavior as their wedding day got closer? Was he spying on Elsie?

A million horrible thoughts collided in her head all at once, exploding in a deadly firebomb nova. Elsie felt violated for learning he wasn't exactly who he always said he was.

Worse, now wasn't the time to ask him questions. Elsie needed to keep her head clear and diffuse this situation.

If only she was wearing underwear. And her pussy soaked from an incomplete orgasm. And if she had a gun.

"Elsie," said Mom. "Do as I say."

"No," Elsie said, not quite regretting her bitchy tone of voice. "Whatever's going on between you and..." She couldn't say the name Molly, not now. "...her, needs to get resolved."

"Oh what a load of crap," Kevin blurted. "What's going on between you and... her?"

"That—that's irrelevant!" said Elsie. "It was nothing!"

"Nothing? Looked like a soaking wet nothing from here."

Mom boxed Kevin on the side of his face. He took the hit like a pro, head bending with the blow, brows furrowed and reddened with anger.

"There's one solution to our mess," said Molly. "Gertie *comes* with me."

The way she said "comes" simultaneously curled Elsie's toes and made her stomach churn.

Mom withdrew her gun, and dropped it into her purse. She stepped around Kevin, putting a hand on his forearm to gently get him to draw down, too.

"Mother!" Elsie said. "You're not seriously going with her?"

"She's right," she said. "This is between me and Molly."

"I won't allow this. I won't let this strange bitch hurt you."

Molly cleared her throat, a happy and light smile spread across her smeared red lips. "Darling, please. I wouldn't dream of hurting Gertie. Much less you."

Molly winked at Elsie, a playful giggle erupted from her throat. She motioned to her goon, Nikolai, to stand down, and offered an arm to Mom.

They walked out arm in arm, a crooked scrunch in Mom's brow. Elsie leaned against the counter, helpless.

Kevin kept his distance, gun still in hand. "Well now," he said. "What's the next move?"

Elsie waited until the front door slammed shut. "Go fuck yourself," she said. She pushed him out of the way and ran downstairs.

CHAPTER EIGHT

KEVIN DIDN'T EXACTLY KNOW WHAT TO DO. Elsie's shove was rough, and a lot stronger than he expected. He shifted his weight, taking the blow with his back foot.

The pitter-patter of her feet on the sandy brown carpet was rapid fire. Shoulders hunched and arms crossed in front of her stomach, face hidden by her hair, Elsie disappeared around the corner downstairs. Kevin wasn't sure if she was crying.

Elsie was pretty talented at holding it in. Better than many men.

They'd had their disputes by now, like when Kevin forgot Elsie's birthday, and when she had mysteriously disappeared without saying a word. Truth was, Elsie being angry at him lifted the weight of his secret a little bit. She couldn't be more angry at him, or if so, at least the camel's back was already broken.

He still couldn't tell her he was a spy, though Elsie deserved the truth. Some secrets had to remain secret, even if they hurt to keep them in.

Kevin stood at the top of the stairs, debating whether to go down and comfort Elsie or not. What was he going to say? Or do, besides pat her on the shoulder and lie about things being alright?

He took each step at a time, every footfall loud as possible to let her know he was coming.

Elsie sat at the minibar, a bottle of Jack Daniels at her elbow and a crystal shot glass in one hand. Niagara Falls ran down her face, along with streaked mascara. She looked like a raccoon.

Kevin waved and plastered a smile on his face. "I'm not angry about..."

...what?

Walking in while a strange woman buried her face in between Elsie's legs? Jealous, maybe. Angry, nope. How could he be angry about that?

But he was angry that the strange woman was no other than the mysterious Biggins who haunted his nightmares.

He cleared his throat and started over. "Wanna talk?"

"No." Elsie poured herself another shot and whisked it back. Her head shook from the stinging burn of alcohol, and she turned away from him.

Kevin touched her shoulder, and she pulled away as if his fingers were on fire.

"We'll find your mother," he offered. "We can..."

Shit, call the authorities? Use his spy talents to get her back? Kevin didn't have an easy answer.

"We'll find her," he said again.

"Blow it out your asshole," said Elsie, cold and calm. Scary calm. She poured another drink.

The drink wasn't for Kevin.

He walked to the billiard table. It was a simple thing to set the balls in the triangle, keep his mind busy while Elsie fumed at him. Kevin had to do something, and wasn't sure what exactly to do besides putz with his hands. He got a stick off the wall, chalked it, and broke the balls.

The hard clattering of balls hitting balls was satisfying.

Pool wasn't his game. Elsie, when they first met, used to believe he allowed her to win. Truth was, Kevin was terrible at angles, and playing in a smoke filled bar while buzzed just made his game worse.

He made three attempts to sink the eight ball before Elsie turned around. She sat askance, legs crossed and sundress riding high up on her thigh. She wasn't wearing panties, far as he knew.

For some dumb reason, that thought made Kevin hard. So he stood behind the billiard table, and bent forward slightly with his palms pressed against the table's rim.

Kevin stared into Elsie's eyes for a long moment. He wanted nothing more than to wipe away the goofy raccoon mascara smudges running down both sides of her face.

Elsie's chin and cheeks got tighter. Fierce. Her brows tightened, and she stared right back at him. The mascara smudges were more like warpaint now.

Great. Now she was buzzed enough to feel brave. Kevin swallowed.

"What the hell," said Elsie, voice gravelly and husky, "is your connection to Biggins?"

"Connection?" said Kevin, knowing his bluff was already called. Elsie was too smart for him. That made her dangerous. Both to him, and to herself.

"Yes," she said. Elsie slid off the barstool and strutted to the billiard table. Palms pressed flat on the table, she faced off with Kevin, giving him a good view of her cleavage. "Your connection. She knew you. And when you realized who she was, I could hear your testicles rolling around on the floor."

"I don't know her at all," Kevin replied. "Not as well as you do, apparently."

Elsie blushed and stood up straighter, and pointed an accusing finger at Kevin. "It was *your* fantasy, mister. Isn't that what you used to tell me?"

"Yeah. But I figured we'd invite another woman to play *together*. Wasn't that the plan?"

"The plan? We're not even married. And you're lecturing me about what I can and can't do?"

"What does that have to do with anything?"

"I'm a single woman! I can have whoever I want between my legs!"

"Maybe I'll find a floozie to play with!"

"Fine!" she said.

"Fine!" he said.

"Fine! But you still didn't answer my question."

"You didn't exactly answer mine."

"You didn't ask one." Elsie leaned forward again, eyes hard as steel. No traces of tears were left. She was all hard boiled, and looked ready to crack his nuts open.

Kevin gripped the pool stick in both hands, sweaty palms slick on the smooth hardwood. "What is *your* relationship with Biggins?"

"I just met the bitch," said Elsie, tone even and cruel. "And she kidnapped my mother for reasons I don't understand." She paused, a lock of hair falling over one brow, which Kevin always found sexy until now. "Your turn."

Kevin walked around the table, breathing slow in and out with each step. He settled one hip on the table, near Elsie's right hand. She still wore the diamond engagement ring he'd given her.

He looked her straight in the eye.

"Biggins blackmailed me," he said. He expected relief to fill him with the confession. Instead, his stomach felt weighed down with rocks. Kevin could hardly breath, waiting for Elsie to say or do something.

He didn't have to wait too long.

Elsie laughed. At first a tiny chuckle, which grew into a full blown belly laugh as if he had told her the dirtiest joke on Earth. Kevin shifted the weight on his hip, not sure what to say next. Not sure what her response meant.

So he put on his best poker face and stayed cool as a cucumber in the fridge.

"You?" she said, gasping for breath. "Blackmailed by Biggins? Good God, why?"

"It's not what you think," said Kevin. *What did she think?* Hell, how would he see the situation if things were turned around? "Look, I've done some bad things. But this one wasn't my fault exactly."

"I hope not," Elsie controlled her laughing at last and swiped the lock of hair behind one ear. "Biggins is the real deal. Bad news. You don't know the shit-storm you poked your head into."

Kevin pulled away from her as if she had bitten him. He would've preferred a bite.

"Wait?" he said. "How do you know Biggins?"

"I don't," Elsie said. "I know things about people."

The way she said it sent a chill down Kevin's arms. As if a curtain had been parted, and a cold stiff breeze blew through. How had it not seen this side of Elsie before? She was being her usual confident self, but different. Creepy, and more than a little mysterious.

He stepped back a step. And another, until his backside hit the wall.

"I think," said Kevin, clearing his throat. "I think we need to come clean with each other."

"Baby," said Elsie, a glint of wicked humor shining in her eyes. "I'm a bad girl."

CHAPTER NINE

HER ENTIRE BODY CLENCHED and tingled hot, her earlier frustration near forgotten. For the moment.

Kevin so much as admitted to be a member of the spy community. Elsie wished he would just cough up the truth, but she wasn't about to let on directly either. But learning what she now knew about Kevin, as good as knowing he was a spy, just made him seem hotter.

Elsie really had been a bad girl her entire life. Now she wanted to show Kevin what she meant by that.

She picked a pool stick off the wall, chalked it slow and sensual while licking her lips, and walked around to his side of the table. Elsie leaned over the table, pressing a hip into him, his body heat searing her through the thin material of her sundress.

"Eight ball," she said. "Left corner pocket."

The ball sank into the left corner.

Kevin looked at her askance, brows tight, his eyes roaming up and down her body. Elsie wanted to squeeze his arm as she strutted behind him to reach the cue ball. She resisted the urge.

He smelled really nice. Like he'd just taken a shower, and then worked out. Just enough cleanliness mixed with sweat. Elsie put a little extra sway in her hips.

"Six," she said. "Right corner."

Again, she made the shot.

"We're both intelligent adults," said Kevin, leaning against the corner of the table. "Why don't we just come clean?"

"I can be clean," said Elsie. She dropped her voice, making it sound husky and sly. "Do you want that?"

"Yeah... Well, yeah."

Elsie pressed her lips together in a tight little grin. This was just like grifting a mark, but—

More fun.

He stood up straighter and cleared his throat. "We both know how this ends," Kevin said.

"Oh?" said Elsie. "Just like we both know I'm going to sink the three right where your nut-sack is."

Elsie leaned down, sticking her ass out. The cool air felt pleasant against her bare, warm skin. She wanted the billiard table cleared. Her pussy lips tingled with anticipation, she already was wet. Not having panties on helped with that.

"I don't see how you can make the shot," said Kevin.

"Want to see?" Elsie bit her bottom lip and struck the cue ball.

The cue hit the five, which ricocheted and hit the three. The three ball fell in the hole, right where she said it would.

"I see," said Kevin. "But maybe instead of playing pool, we should worry about your mother."

"She's more dangerous than me," Elsie tossed her hair to one side. "And besides, I don't have a plan yet."

Kevin shifted his weight, gripping the pool stick in both hands. "Maybe we should come up with a plan?"

"So hasty." Elsie called another shot. "Six in the middle pocket."

Again, the ball fell in. She kept making shot after shot, near silence settling on the room. The only sounds were her calls and the satisfying smacking of billiard balls. Kevin grunted now and then, throwing in a "nice shot" or "when will it be my turn" every so often.

They didn't need to say much. Kevin's eyes said it all. Just like the time they walked along the Seine River in Paris. Or when he took to her favorite ice cream stand in Brooklyn. Those sexy brown eyes devoured her up and down, and Elsie reveled in the attention.

And his attention was so much different than the corporate pigs she stole secrets from. They only wanted a piece of ass, or a bitch in a leather outfit to smack them around. A special few professed true love to her, but without an exception they were playing behind a wife's or a girlfriend's back.

Kevin appeared so helpless and weak when he stared at her like this. Like he wanted to spill his guts with secrets. Well, that was certainly true, as she now found out.

But he also looked like a man who would do anything for her, whether he got laid or not. Kevin controlled his lust, this time hiding behind that pool stick as if it would save him from Elsie. The bulge in his pants and the wild eyed expression on his face gave him away.

Elsie had him wrapped around her finger, and she knew it, just like she knew she'd win this pool game.

She sank the last ball.

"Do you use your charms?" Kevin said. "When you're in the field. Please be honest."

"Yes," she said. "But I'll give all that up. For you."

"Can you? Give it up and walk away?"

Elsie meant to say yes again, but hesitated. It wasn't that simple. Once a spy, always a spy. Sometimes, hell all of the time, you didn't get to walk away because you had a change of heart.

"I understand," Kevin said. "I want to give it up for you, too. But I don't know how to get out."

Elsie nodded. Her heart sank, but not exactly because of what Kevin said. The heat between her legs cooled a little. She didn't know how to get out of the business either. Start over. Clean slate.

"I love you," she said. Elsie stepped closer to him, enough to feel his body heat.

"I love you, too," he said. "Just that—"

"Shh," Elsie put a finger to his lips. She traced down the rough stubble on his chin, down his neck, to the button on his polo shirt.

She kissed him. Just a taste. The heat between her legs returned, full blast now. Elsie cuddled up to him, wrapping an arm around his neck.

Kevin pulled her in closer, hands firmly pressed on her waist. He French kissed her, tongues wrestling and probing each other's teeth.

Then he lifted her dress up and cupped her butt in both hands.

All of her insides knotted up pleasurably. Elsie had forgotten how good he felt, how powerful his arms were, and how wonderful it was to snuggle against him and drive him crazy with kissing.

She snapped the shirt's button loose, revealing a patch of wiry chest hair.

Before she realized what she was doing, Elsie was down on her knees and unzipping his pants.

The problems with Zack and Molly faded to background noise. Elsie still wanted to make sure her mother was okay.

But what was Elsie going to do? Chase Molly Biggins through the small town streets of Wenakaga?

Mom could handle herself. Besides, she went willingly with Biggins.

Right now, Elsie needed to handle Kevin.

She yanked his belt buckle hard enough to make him grunt. He didn't stop her. Just stared into her eyes with that wild, helpless expression.

In a flash, his pants were open and his cock sprung free, half hard and wet on the end. She took the head into her mouth, and licked his saltiness clean.

Kevin ran his fingers through her hair, pulling her closer. Elsie grabbed his wrists, and denied him with soft licks along the side of his member. He moaned.

She nibbled at him, play biting up and down the shaft. On the way down, she went lower, and took one ball into her mouth, sucking hard as she could. He jerked away, but the desperate moan told her he wanted more.

So Elsie took the other ball and licked it up, sucking it into her mouth. His cock throbbed to full erection.

Just like she knew would happen.

Elsie kissed and bit back up his shaft, patting him under the sack along the way. Kevin was leaning over now, hands on her shoulders and massaging her.

When she reached the fat mushroom head, Elsie gripped him and took him into her mouth. She twisted her hand as she sucked him, gently scraping her teeth up and down his length.

Right when his moaning grew the most intense, and right before he could climax, Elsie pulled away. She smiled up at him, luxuriating in his musky smell.

"Your turn," she said.

"But," Kevin said, trying to hide his goofy smile, "isn't there some rule that a man can't his bride before the wedding?"

"Fuck the rules, baby. We're not exactly a normal couple anymore."

As if they ever were.

Kevin gripped her upper arms and lifted Elsie to her feet.

Then he went down on her.

CHAPTER TEN

KEVIN SMOOTHED BACK HER SILKY SOFT HAIR. He felt the sweat trickling at the nape of her neck. Elsie hadn't lied when she told him she was bad.

Maybe not in the way she meant it. She was saying she was spy after all? Was she spying on him? Logic told him that was a possibility.

Logic was a cold hearted bitch. Kevin didn't care about logic or thinking right now. And after Elsie pulled open his belt and started slobbering all his manhood, it was too late, spy or not.

Kevin didn't even care about the silly rule about a groom not seeing the bride before the wedding. He kept secrets for a living. No big deal to keep this secret too.

She already smelled like an orgasm, and not from the earlier fling she had in the kitchen. All his will went into not bucking his hips into her face. He enjoyed the rising tension as she sucked him, giving her all the power to tease and get him off. He wanted to enjoy that sensation for as long as possible.

When Kevin couldn't take it any longer, he grabbed Elsie by the upper arms and brought her to her feet. He pushed her into the corner, near the pool stick rack. Sweat trickled down his back, his palms hot and sticky on her smooth arms. A wild, mock-fearful expression plastered Elsie's face—wide eyes, neck and cheeks blushed, mouth in a lovely "O" shape.

Kevin got down on one knee, and lifted her dress above her hips.

Elsie's pussy was shaved into a thin landing strip, just the way he liked it. The hair seemed to point from her navel down to her honey pot. But the shaved areas hadn't been tended to in a few days. The bare skin was rough and bristly.

He dived right in, tongue extended and eager to taste, splitting her lips apart with index and middle fingers. Her clitoris popped out right away, and he licked and nibbled on her pearl.

Elsie combed her fingers through his hair, and pulled as she moaned in ecstasy.

She was gushing wet with juices trickling down both thighs.

Not stopping to give her a rest, not even bothering to tease like he loved doing to her, he sank two fingers inside while he flicked her clit with his tongue. Back and forth, up and down. Kevin wiggled his fingers inside.

Then he curled his fingers into a "come hither" motion, rubbing on her G-spot.

Elsie thrashed against him, knees buckling and fingers pulling his hair tighter. Her hips bucked wildly as she rode his fingers, her essence dripping down his forearm now. Kevin didn't stop, not even slowing, giving her no satisfaction of rest. He rubbed, flicked, and licked every sensitive part of her.

She let out a ferocious holler, shrieking like a sex starved banshee. Breasts bouncing under her dress, her eyes slitted and she threw her head back for another loud moan.

Kevin touched himself, rubbing the slick precum gushing out and slowly stroking down the shaft to his balls. He was so sensitive, his cock hurt with pleasure. He felt the subtle pain deep in his stomach and hips and down his thighs. The tension was sweet and cruel.

He got to his feet.

"No," Elsie whimpered, lips puckered and shoulders bunched up. "No. No, no."

Kevin lightly kissed her on the lips. "Yes."

"No?" A wicked grin burst out across Elsie's pretty mouth. She shook her head, hair loose and waving with the motion.

He leaned in, mouth to her earlobe. He kissed her ear, and tugged ever so gently with his lips. "Yes."

Elsie giggled as if Kevin had told the world's worst dirty joke. She wrapped her arms around his neck, pulling him in. Kevin kissed her jaw, working his way to her chin, finding her lips.

He grabbed her by the waist and roughly jerked her away from the corner. Elsie grunted, the grin and giggles not going away. He flipped her around, away from him so her butt rubbed up against his oh-so-sensitive cock. The wispy material of the sundress sent shivers through him, almost enough to make him lose his load.

She turned her head, tucking her hair away from her face, and winked.

Kevin nudged her to the billiard table, and bent her at the waist. Elsie complied with his wishes, not fighting, just going with the flow and letting him have his way. Her ass poked out of the sundress, perky and round and so lovely.

He smacked her on the ass.

Once on one cheek. Another time on the other.

A crazy little laugh erupted from Elsie. She buried her head between her arms and wiggled her backside, trying to get closer to Kevin.

One more smack. Loud and crisp and sharp.

Elsie moaned.

And then Kevin entered her, balls deep into her slick tunnel.

He pumped her with long and slow strokes, building the tension between them. Sweet, exquisite torture. Elsie grinded her hips on him, pressing hard against his pelvis.

Her body glistened with sweat now. The sundress clung to her like a second skin. She panted for breath.

Kevin grabbed a fistful of hair and yanked her head back. He rammed her now, faster.

Balls slapping against her skin, Kevin burned like a flame tossed on gasoline. Breathing became harder. Short gasps. Every pump divinely aching. Muscles burning from the workout.

Elsie clenched around his cock. Wet, juicy spurts flowed down his balls. She slapped the table top and screamed.

Kevin couldn't hold back anymore.

He gripped her waist in both hands, holding her still as he could. His cock ached from tip to base, and down into his balls.

Kevin came inside his fiancee. One spurt after another.

Pulling out hurt. He was so sensitive.

He leaned against the wall and wiped his forehead with both hands. His cock twitched, aching for more but exhausted from what he just had. Breathing in and out, chest puffed out. He felt invincible.

Elsie didn't move, head cradled in her arms.

Kevin touched her on the hip. Elsie cooed, something between a moan and a gurgle. He rubbed her lower back, working his way up. To her shoulders, massaging.

She pushed herself up.

And fell into his chest and arms.

He held her, and basked in the afterglow. Elsie looked up at him, her breathing slow and steady now.

"I still love you," she said. "Even if you're a dirty spy."

"Good," Kevin said. "Because I'm madly in love with you."

"I was serious about doing bad things. And I don't really mean sexually."

"None of us are innocent."

They fell silent. Kevin wanted to lie down with her. But dread overtook him—the blackmail, the impending wedding, Biggins—wiping away the perfect warm feeling of intimacy.

Kevin pushed Elsie away.

"I have things to do," he said. Kevin picked up his clothes and walked away. The air conditioning felt suddenly cold against his naked skin.

CHAPTER ELEVEN

ELSIE DID NOT WANT TO WASH OFF the musky smell of sex. Of Kevin. Any other day, she would've let the odor cling to her all day as she went about her daily activities.

But not today.

She took an afternoon shower. After she turned off the water, she could hear Kevin walking around upstairs. Pacing, back and forth. Elsie thought about his reaction, when she told him she loved him. Of course he returned the sweet words, and made it sound like he meant it.

He was a professional spy after all. That's what he did. Lied for a living.

Or rather, what Elsie did for a living. She still wasn't sure exactly what it was Kevin did. If she'd ever get to find out.

But then, after proclaiming his love, he turned and walked away, shoulders slumped and head bowed. Not at all looking like a man who just had wild sex with the woman he loves.

What did it mean?

Elsie dried off quick and streaked nude across the hall to the downstairs guest bedroom. Her luggage was there. She grabbed a set of lacy black bra and panties, a black sleeveless blouse, and jeans. She didn't bother drying her hair, or with makeup.

She walked upstairs with her strappy wedge sandals in hand. Kevin was at the dinette table, with a stack of Mom's magazines at his elbow. He read the January edition of *Red Book.*

"Engaging read?" Elsie said, not trying real hard to hide her smirk.

"Amazing what you can learn from the lady mags," said Kevin.

"Such as?"

He hid his face behind the magazine, peering over the top at her as if sharing the world's dirtiest secret. "Ten ways to improve your sex life."

"I remember that article! Pretty solid advice, if I recall correctly."

"Or how about the one on five ways to tell he's not really into you."

"Also solid advice. Saved me more than a few times."

"Oh?"

"Yeah."

"You going to tell me about that?"

"How about you blab first," said Elsie. "You mind telling me why you're in big trouble with Miss Biggins?"

Kevin sighed and tossed the *Red Book* aside, avoiding eye contact with Elsie. The color in his cheeks blanched. He sat still, hardly moving a muscle except for a nervous tap-tap-tapping of his forefinger.

Elsie opened her mouth to say something—anything to break the awkward silence—and then words came out of his mouth too, overlapping with her words and making a garbled mess of sound.

"Go ahead," she said, and sat on the red cushioned barstool next to him.

"Ever wonder," Kevin said. He shifted his butt on his stool. "Ever wonder if we're not meant to be?"

Elsie grabbed his hand, a little to roughly perhaps, but she had to stop the annoying little tapping. Then she squeezed his hand and put on a pleasant smile.

"All the time," she said. "Baby, I worried about being with you constantly from the day we met."

"You did a good job at hiding that worry," Kevin said.

"I'm sorry. I just wanted a normal life, without intrigues and danger. I wanted to be a housewife and join a bookclub and garden or whatever the fuck normal suburban people do."

"I wanted that, too." Kevin adjusted his collar, and looked her in the eyes. "Well, not being the housewife part. But you know."

"Yeah, I know."

She wanted to add so much. To say things to make him feel better, to comfort him, win him back. Hell, Elsie wanted to talk to comfort herself. But she let the silence hang. It was a sweet moment of tension.

She'd have preferred the tension of rough sex.

Kevin tapped with his other finger.

She grabbed his other hand, and squeezed tight once.

"I don't have this nervous tick in the field," Kevin said at last. "Just seems to happen with you."

Elsie had noticed the habit, often when Kevin was trying to hide something. Like when he proposed, but he tried waiting until the "perfect moment" to pop the question.

It'd been at Ned's Bistro, a pasta and lasagna joint in New York City. The tapping drove Elsie near insane, until she grabbed him by the hands, much like she was doing now, and peppered him question after question.

He broke down, got on one knee, and presented her with the most beautiful diamond ring she had ever seen.

Elsie had often wondered if he were a spy, but that nervous tick told her he was a normal guy. A confident, sweet talking guy, but just a guy. She'd been wrong.

What else had Kevin been hiding all this time?

She clutched his hands, tickling his palms with her fingernails. The skin was sweaty and warm. If he knew what to look for, he'd also note how sweaty and warm her palms were. At least that made them even, Elsie hoped.

Time to ask the tough questions.

"What is Biggins blackmailing you for?" Elsie asked. She couldn't call the woman "Molly." Not after the oral Elsie received from her. Molly Biggins was good with her tongue and lips, the thought of which made Elsie wet again.

She squeezed her legs shut, trying not think of either Biggins or Kevin going down on her.

"It's complicated," said Kevin.

"Look," Elsie said. "If we're going to go face off with her, I need to know what she wants from you. The more you tell me, the more I can help you."

"I doubt it. I can't be saved."

"That's not helping." The tone of her voice came out more harsh, more critical than she intended. Elsie let go of his hands, and balled hers into fists. Every nerve in her body felt raw. Too many surprises, too much random sex, for one day.

Elsie wanted a nap. She wasn't even sure she wanted to know whatever Kevin's deep, dark secret he was holding in.

But she needed to find her mother soon, before the day was done. Elsie would not be able to sleep tonight if she didn't do something.

She needed weapons to fight Biggins.

"Kevin, sweetie," she said. Elsie took a deep breath. "I know this is hard, trusting other people for help. But you got to trust me. Okay?"

God, who was she to say high and mighty things about trust?

Kevin wiped his forehead and face with both hands. He sighed. "Do you know what business Biggins really is in?"

"No."

"Puppies."

"What?" *What the fuck?*

"You heard me," Kevin said. "Puppies. She operates a puppy mill network throughout the States and Canada. It's a cover for other things she does, like weapons smuggling and such. But her primary crime is puppy mills."

"Okay." Elsie wasn't sure if she wanted to laugh or slap Kevin for being such a good liar. Far as she could tell, he was telling the truth.

"I know it sounds like bullshit," he said. "But it's true."

"Then how did you..."

Kevin leaned forward, and touched her forearm. His fingertips were warm and tender. "I used to spy for a puppy chow corporation."

"Okay." Elsie had a hard time thinking of a more appropriate response to what he was saying. She cleared her throat. "Those puppy mills must've been lucrative for your bosses."

"Exactly." Kevin rubbed her forearm. He looked her in the eyes. "Stealing dog food recipes was boring work. I wanted out."

"I can understand."

"So I revealed the puppy mill chain to a rival corporation. It felt like the right thing to do before I moved on to new work. But somehow Biggins learned about me. She wanted money at first, and then she threatened to out me to my new bosses."

"So let me guess. She's had you in her pocket ever since?"

"Yup. I know, stupid story. But I've never gotten rid of her. I didn't even know she was a female until today. And today she sent an email, demanding the rest of the money she wants."

Elsie touched Kevin on the cheek. She bit her lip, trying to hold back a laugh that demanded to be released. Stealing puppy chow recipes? Puppy mills? Elsie would've killed to have such ludicrous problems. The Wall Street executives she seduced for a job were vicious assholes.

Dog food makers sounded... quaint.

Her cell phone buzzed. A text message.

A picture from her mother, of a brown wooden sign that read "Mendota Bluffs" in white paint and an arrow.

"I know where Mom is," said Elsie. "Let's go."

CHAPTER TWELVE

KEVIN SHIFTED THE LASABRE IN GEAR and drove five miles over the speed limit to Mendota Bluffs. It wasn't far, and would've made a lovely walk if money and potentially lives weren't at stake.

Hands on the wheel and eyes laser-focused on the road, Kevin pretended to be in the zone. Truth was, he felt sweet relief from talking with Elsie, and that was mildly distracting. For so long he'd worried Elsie wouldn't understand him, that she would forever be an outsider to his inner world.

Instead, Kevin had found a kindred spirit.

Someone who could relate to the difficulties and treacheries of the spy world. Kevin was on cloud nine.

The feeling of being understood both excited and scared him at the same time.

Unfortunately, he had Biggins to thank for how he found out the truth about Elsie. He didn't know if he'd ever find out the entire truth about Elsie. But the spy business was hard with all the secrets, and both she and Kevin could mutually understand the need for such secrets.

He only wished the blackmail would go away, so he could be truly happy for his upcoming wedding. At least he hoped Elsie still wanted to marry him.

She said something. She sat with one hand hand in her lap, and the opposite elbow resting on the windowsill.

"Say what?" Kevin asked.

"You're going to miss the turn!" Elsie snapped, pointing at the street he was supposed to turn at, nag-voice on full blast.

Kevin slammed the brakes and spun the wheel lightening quick. The tires screeched as the Buick spun 270 degrees. Elsie pressed her palms flat against the dashboard. Heart pounding in his head, Kevin righted the car with a fast turn of the wheel and a gentle tap on the accelerator.

"Well," Elsie said, sarcastic venom dripping from her words, "there goes the element of surprise."

She stared at him through slitted eyes, face red and not at all pleased looking.

Kevin smirked like a boy with a shoebox full of captured lizards. Yes, he was happy, all things considered. But why did the day have to be such a rollercoaster?

"Do you have a gun?" he asked.

"Yes," said Elsie. "No. Never mind. Can I borrow one of yours?"

"What do you mean, yes but no?"

"Have a gun. But not on me."

"You don't carry a spare?"

"Fuck it, Kev. How many hiding places do you think lady's clothes have?"

"What makes you think I have a spare?" Damn it! Kevin had a spare in his ankle holster, a 9mm. Did he trust Elsie enough to lend it to her?

"Do you know a guy named Zack Gibbs?" said Elsie.

"No," said Kevin. "Wait. Is he on the guest list?"

The list was short. Basically friends and family. Neither Kevin nor Elsie had much family, which made sense now. Spies tend to cut ties early on in their career, just something that happens. Kevin had wondered why Elsie only had a mother and a small circle of friends. For a long while, she didn't even have a maid-of-honor, which surprised Kevin at the time.

"If you see Zack," said Elsie, "shoot him for me, will you? You'll recognize him by the douchey leer he gives me."

"Will do."

Kevin pulled into the parking lot at the base of Mendota Bluffs. A wooden "Welcome" sign graced the entrance. Only two other cars were in the lot, one was a Lincoln Towncar, the other a red GTO convertible. At least the park would be quiet. Fewer bystanders, the better.

Kevin bent down and unholstered the 9mm. "Here," he said. "Take it."

"Thank you," said Elsie. She weighed the gun in her hand, and then slipped it in her front pocket, under her blouse. "It's similar to my Smith & Wessen."

"Glad you appreciate it."

"A lady should know her guns," she squeezed his thigh and glanced down at his lap. "Of all kinds."

A little tingle shot through Kevin, making him feel warm. He smiled, and thought about leaning forward to kiss her. Just a peck on the mouth, to show her how he appreciated her.

But they had other things to do.

He got out of the car.

All business now, they walked across the hot black top parking lot to the trail that wound up to the bluffs. Kevin wanted to hold Elsie's hand, comfort her. Seemed the romantic thing to do when hiking on a nature trail.

But he resisted the urge, and simply walked close to her shoulder. For her protection, of course.

"Why did Biggins take your mother here?" he asked.

"I don't know," Elsie said. She peered at him from her periphery, behind her hair. "I used to go up this trail as a kid. To get away."

"Your mother know you up here?"

"Probably. No telling what she knew. Hell, the woman was a spy long before I even knew what that meant. I'm sure she knows more about my private youth life than I care to remember."

"Such as?"

"What's with the twenty questions, mister?" Elsie nudged him with her elbow, a crooked grin gracing her lips.

Kevin nudged back, gently but enough to unbalance her in her wedge sandals. Elsie staggered, arms flailing and a light-hearted giggle accidentally escaping. Kevin caught her by the upper arm and righted her.

She pressed a hand against his chest, sighed, and then pushed him away.

"Come on," she said. "Mom could be in trouble."

"You're right," said Kevin, hands held out. "I'm professional now."

He checked his pistol in the holster, and straightened his jacket.

"Good." Elsie turned and headed up the dirt and wood-chip trail. She was a sight to see, hiking up a hill in wedges. She didn't seem to think too much of it.

Kevin's patent leather shoes weren't much better, but at least he had some support. The shoes would need a lot of polish afterwards, if they could even be salvaged.

The trail wound through a thick forest of pine and maple trees, the canopy thick enough to block out the late afternoon sunlight. It was like walking into a church with high vaulted ceilings, being closed in from the outside yet still communing with the larger world.

Kevin tried to walk quiet, but the trail had far too many twigs that snapped with each step. Elsie was right about the element of surprise being gone.

The trail got steeper, winding criss-cross back and forth up the bluff.

Voices were up ahead. Kevin tapped Elsie on the shoulder, finger to his mouth. He pointed ahead, and she nodded. They stopped to listen, but the voices were too far away and the words hardly decipherable.

So they climbed slower now. Kevin got out his gun, and held it behind his back. Elsie checked to make sure the 9mm was still in her pocket, but she didn't draw.

The voices got closer. Up ahead, through the trees and around the bend in the trail, was Gertrude, Biggins, and Nikolai. A shovel was stuck in the ground near the big man in the badly tailored suit.

"Where is it Gertie?" said Molly Biggins, a rough and impatient edge to her accent.

"Do you expect me to remember this after five years?" Gertrude's voice. She sounded tired, but confident. A little cocky.

"Da. I am surprised at your ineptitude, darling."

Kevin grabbed Elsie by the wrist and led her further up the trail. Closer to trouble. They walked even slower, almost a crawl, avoiding every stick in the path.

"Look," Gertrude said loudly. "There's a lot of damn trees up here. Give me a minute to find it."

"I love you, darling," said Biggins. "But things will get ugly if you don't."

A revolver clicked. And then a second. Kevin could see Nikolai and Biggins both holding guns at Gertrude now.

Kevin drew his pistol and stepped in front of Elsie, holding an arm out to keep her back.

He ran. Blood and adrenaline pumped through his brain. His thighs burned from the uphill exertion.

Gertrude, Biggins, and Nikolai were standing in a clearing that overlooked sleepy Wenakaga.

Kevin leaped around the corner, out of cover.

"Kevin!" Elsie yelled. "Watch out!"

Too late. Kevin was already committed to his action. He ran even faster.

He stopped just at the edge of the clearing.

And then he felt the muzzle of a gun behind his head.

And the click of a bullet being loaded in the chamber.

Shit.

CHAPTER THIRTEEN

THE PRACTICAL THING WOULD'VE BEEN to take off her wedge sandals before running up the incline to the bluff. But that would've taken precious seconds.

The even more practical thing would've been to wear actual shoes.

Far too late now.

Elsie was fit and strong, but her calves and ankles were going to pay for this later. She ran after Kevin, who got the not-so-smart idea to jump into the fray and be a hero.

She felt a little weak in the knees watching her man be bold and confident. Heat swelled between her thighs as she charged after him. If he didn't get shot, she'd make passionate love to him all over again.

But that was later.

Right now, everyone in sight had a gun.

Out of the corner of her vision, she saw a glimmer of red pop out from behind a tree. A blond haired man in a red jogging suit.

He also had a gun. Her Smith & Wessen 9mm.

Elsie yelled for Kevin to watch out.

Once again, she was too late.

The man in red put the gun behind Kevin's head.

"Zack!" Elsie shouted, pointing her borrowed gun at him. "You ass douche! Back off from my fiancee!" Molly Biggins and Nikolai pointed their guns at Mom, who had her hands in the air. Kevin had Biggins in his sights.

Elsie was ready to shoot Zack a new asshole.

And take back the gun he stole, not to mention the dirty pictures he took with his cell phone.

"*Back off my fiancee,*" mumbled Zack, confident sarcasm oozing off his words. "Make me, bitch."

"Just what the hell do you think you're doing here?" Elsie said, voice shaking. She was losing her cool, and she knew it. A warm breeze blowing in the wrong direction could set her off, and make her pull her trigger finger. Elsie didn't want it to come to that.

But every nerve in her body tingled with energy, as if somebody lit a fuse to a bomb and she had only a few seconds left before it blew up.

"Molly, baby," Zack said. "You look fantastic. Love the white suit. Makes you stand out in the woods more."

Odd thing coming from a man in a bold red jogging suit. Fuck! How did Elsie not see him coming?

Biggins shifted her aim from Mom to Zack and, unfortunately, Kevin who was in the way.

"Darling," she said. "Zack? Is it? I have to ask the same question as my dear *friend*, Elsie."

With the word "friend," Biggins curled her lip in a cruel Elvis-style pout, and winked. Elsie wanted to vomit.

"Collecting debts," said Zack. "One from you," he pointed Elsie's gun at Mom. "Another from you," pointing at Biggins.

"I owe you nothing," Biggins hissed.

"And one from you, baby," Zack pointed the gun at Elsie. He slapped Kevin on the shoulder. "Sorry bro, you're the odd man out today."

"You owe me," Elsie said, finger on the trigger.

"Easy there, girl," said Zack. "Don't blow your load yet. We can do this the easy way, before someone does something stupid."

Elsie gritted her teeth. And then lowered her gun, slightly. She exchanged glances with Biggins, and Mom, and then nodded to Zack.

"Good," he said. "First things first. Both of you," he pointed at Elsie and Kevin, "drop you guns and kick them away. Now."

Elsie held out one hand, and bent her knees. A lump in her throat, she clicked the safety on, and tossed the gun on ground. And then kicked it toward Zack. She nodded to Kevin.

He followed her example, and tossed his gun behind him to Zack.

"Okay, okay," said Zack, pointing off to his side. "Lovebirds, go over there for a minute."

Elsie went to where Zack pointed, a few steps away from Molly Biggins. Elsie ignored the blond woman's quirky leer. Biggins still smelled like fresh pussy.

Kevin stood next to Elsie. "I don't have an extra gun," he whispered.

"Don't worry," Elsie whispered back.

"Hey kids!" Zack said, training his gun on them both. "Cut the chatter for after class. Now you," he aimed his gun at Biggins, "I want the black book."

Biggins chuckled, her whole body shaking with laughter as if it were coming from the bottom of her toes.

"You?" she said. "Want the black book? What?"

"Don't argue with me, skank. Just hand it over."

"I said *nyet*. I don't think you know what you're asking for."

"Money, power, secrets. I don't care what's in the book. I want it. And now."

"Well you can't have it."

Mom stepped forward, a weird smile on her lips. The same smile she got when she used to trick Elsie into eating her vegetables.

"I think you should give it to him," Mom said.

"Have you fallen off your rocker?" Biggins said. "You'd pay the price too, if he got hold of the black book."

"Maybe. But so what? I've got my family to think of. Elsie and... umm, Kevin."

"Do you *remember* where you hid it now?"

"Yeah," said Mom. "It's buried under the tree right behind you."

Biggins snapped her fingers and pointed at the tree. "Nikolai. Dig."

The big man with the scar got the shovel and started digging, grunting as he worked. He broke a sweat by the time the shovel hit something hard and metallic.

While everyone was distracted by the digging, Kevin reached over and held Elsie's hand. She squeezed, and he squeezed back. The day had gone from bad to weird to just flat embarrassing. At least she still had her Kevin.

Nikolai knelt down lifted a metal lockbox out of the earth.

"Finally," said Biggins. She took a key out of her pocket. "It better still be in here, Gertie."

"I certainly haven't touched," said Mom.

Kevin leaned over to Elsie's ear, his body heat close and warm, comforting her. "Do you know what this is about?"

"No clue," whispered Elsie.

Biggins opened the lockbox, and took out a brown paper bag wrapped around something book-shaped. She opened the bag and looked inside.

"Still here," she said. "After all these years. And you kept your word, Gertie."

"You had doubts?" said Mom. "Look, you want it so bad, have it. Those years are behind me."

Biggins pouted. "You don't mean to say—"

"I mean exactly that. It's over."

"Okay." Biggins wiped a hand across her face. Her eyes were red and her mascara smeared. She looked ready to bawl.

"Hey, cry babies," Zack said, and put his gun to Elsie's head. "Hand it over. Make it choppy."

Kevin clenched his jaw tight, veins popping in his throat and forehead. Elsie clenched his hand.

"Molly," said Mom. "The black book isn't that important. It's just a book."

Biggins nodded, wiping away the tears on her cheeks. She kissed the paper bag, and handed it to Zack.

"See," Zack said. "That wasn't so hard. Elsie, baby, thanks again for the lovely photos. You remember my room number?"

"Honey," said Kevin. "What photos?"

"I'll see you in hell," said Elsie.

"Your loss," said Zack. "But you should know Mr. Dudley Do-right is a cheater."

"Excuse me?" Elsie and Kevin said at the same time.

"Yeah," Zack puffed his chest up. "You should see the bridal suite. He had some skanks over last night. Wow, I heard the bed shaking until the wee hours of the morning. Woo-wee!"

"Kevin!" Elsie pulled away her hand and backed up as if she had found a snake. "How— How could you?"

"It's a lie," said Kevin.

Elsie pushed him. Hard. Towards the edge of the bluff. Blood pumped through her head, making her feel light and woozy. And angry as hell.

"Well, later assholes," said Zack, holding the paper bag up for everyone to see. "Love you, Elsie."

He jogged away back down the trail.

Elsie pushed Kevin again. Closer to the edge.

"How could you!" she shouted. Elsie just wished she could come up with something better to say, but deep, hot-boiled anger kept her from thinking right.

Mom touched on the shoulder. "Elsie, dear."

Elsie pulled away. Her vision narrowed to a tunnel. Everything seemed to happen in slow motion. She felt almost almost out of body, as if staring down from above the treetops.

She felt out of control.

Kevin was so close to the edge, his face so nervous and scared. Just a step closer. She didn't even have to touch him again.

Kevin slipped off the edge.

And fell feet first.

He grabbed onto the rocky edge with his fingers.

"Elsie," he said. "Help!"

"We were almost married!" Elsie said. "And you cheated!"

Feeling oddly like a Vaudeville villain but with anger issues, she stepped on his fingers.

"How dare you!" she yelled.

CHAPTER FOURTEEN

KEVIN HADN'T REALIZED HOW CLOSE TO THE EDGE he was. How close Elsie had pushed him.

Her face contorted and pinched, hell-bent angry. She was red as a lobster.

He tried telling her, calmly as possible, that Zack had lied. The back of Kevin's neck felt hot and sticky. His armpits felt glued to his shirt.

Elsie took more step towards him.

He took a step back.

And then slipped.

Loose rocks and crunchy gravel fell underneath his foot.

The fall almost certainly bruised his stomach. His ribcage hurt bad. Probably not broken, but the pain stung fierce. His heart raced up his throat, making him want to vomit. He dared not look down. The sheer nothingness under his feet gave him enough vertigo.

Somehow he had grabbed on the ledge. And Elsie stepped her clunky wedge sandals on his fingers.

"Elsie!" Kevin said, panic quavering on the surface like a shark fin above the waves. "Baby, listen! He lied!"

"How could you!" she yelled, grinding her toe on his fingers. Pain shot threw every nerve in his hand, all the way up his elbow. He gritted his teeth, tasting loose sand and dirt.

Kevin dug his feet onto the rock, trying to find something to step onto. Unlike a rock climbing wall, the ledge of Mendota Bluff was smooth with no hand-holds he could find. And his shoes had no traction on the bottom.

Every muscle in his body strained and burned. He wasn't going to last long.

"Elsie, please help me! I love only you!"

"Did you say that to those floozies last night? Huh?" Elsie grinded her foot on his other hand.

Gertrude, worry mixed with grim determination on her face, put a hand on her daughter's shoulder. Elsie pulled away.

And then spat.

Her loogie landed square in Kevin's right eye. Half his vision gone and blurry with warm spit, Kevin kept staring at her. Part disbelief, part utter terror.

"Elsie!" yelled Gertrude.

So this was how it ended? Being pushed off a cliff by the woman he loved? Sure, he knew all along Elsie had anger management issues. And she wasn't a saint by any means. Why the hell did Kevin want to marry her anyway?

Looking up at Elsie—long denim clad legs, bare tanned arms, black hair blowing in the wind—Kevin imagined her as the angel of death. The last woman most guys ever wanted to see.

And he was in love.

Not despite her ferocious temper and scary fighting spirit. Rather, because of it. What other woman could live with a spy, but another spy?

Then he thought about the last time they made love, in Elsie's mother's basement just a short time ago. Why couldn't it have been somewhere nicer?

Like the bridal suite?

"Elsie!" Gertrude yelled again.

Kevin dug his fingernails in the rock and squeezed, lifting himself up. His arms ached too much. Acid was building up in his muscles. His hands wanted to let go, relax. Kevin fought with all his strength to hang on.

Mouth a thin cruel thin line, Elsie stomped on his fingers, hard. It felt as if every bone in his hand snapped, crackled, and popped. Sharp pain shot up his arm.

"Elisa Patricia Turner!" Gertrude pinched Elsie on the shoulder.

Elsie half turned. "Mom?"

"I was at the bridal suite earlier today," said Gertrude. "The room was a mess. But no floozies."

"What?" The vinegar gone from Elsie's voice. "Really?"

"Yes, honey. Kevin is a good man."

"But..."

Kevin grunted, redoubling his effort to hang on for life. He hung by the fingernails, if the wind blew the wrong way and unbalanced him anymore...

"Elsie," he said. "Who do you trust? Me? Or Zack?"

Her face slackened, shoulders slumped, Elsie put a hand to her mouth. Calm realization settled on her brow, as if a lightbulb got turned on over her head. Kevin and Elsie shared a long look that only lasted a half second.

He was half blind and fighting the urge to wipe the spit out of his eye.

She narrowed her eyes to slits, fire lighting her face.

After that long half second, Elsie squatted down and clutched Kevin by the wrist with her sweat soaked hands.

"Baby," she said. "I got you."

"Don't let go," said Kevin.

"I won't." Elsie pulled, the veins in her neck throbbing with the strain.

Gertrude knelt down, too, and grabbed his other wrist. Molly joined in, on the other side of Elsie, pulling.

Kevin kicked and grunted his way up. All three women heaved, lifting him inch by inch.

Nikolai laid a big, sweaty hand on the Kevin's collar. Like picking up a kitten by the scruff of the neck, Nikolai sighed and lifted.

Kevin moaned in relief when his knees scraped against the rough, rocky upside of the bluff.

He landed in Elsie's arms. She pulled him close, wrapped him tight against her bosom, wiping away her spit with a thumb.

"I'm sorry," she said, on the edge of sobbing, patting one hand on his hair. "I'm sorry. So sorry."

"You're—" said Kevin. "Stop... choking... me..."

Elsie let go and held him at arm's length. "Oh. Sorry about that, too."

"You can also stop apologizing," he said. He pressed a finger to her mouth while he caught his breath. "Seriously. I can't explain it."

"Me either," Elsie said. "Wait? What?"

"You almost killed me. I should be angry about that. But I'm not."

Elsie laughed, a nervous jitter shaking her body, and pulled away from him. She pressed her hands against her eyes, trying and failing to stop the water works.

"But why? I'm a psycho. And you're a nice guy who used to sell puppy chow recipes."

"I know. But that's not what—"

Elsie stood up, hands out as if to keep pushing Kevin away. "I don't deserve you. You deserve a girl who won't axe murder you in your sleep."

Kevin stayed on his knees and crawled to Elsie. He took her by the hands.

"But that's where you're wrong," he said.

"Or blow your head off with a shotgun if you come home five hours too late."

"Umm, Elsie..."

"Or push you off a cliff. Oh God! Kevin!" Elsie snapped her hands away and hugged herself, crying and rocking on her heels.

Kevin got off his knees. He grabbed her by the shoulders, a bit too rough, but he didn't care anymore. He only cared about one thing.

He shook her. When she didn't stop crying, he dug his fingernails in her skin and shook her again like a rag-doll. Elsie's hair hung over her face, partially hiding her. Kevin swept her hair aside, and held her head.

"I put my life at risk every time I go on a mission to steal corporate secrets on Wall Street. I'm not dodging bullets or escaping bombs, but it's a short life nonetheless."

"I know," said Elsie, sniffling. "That's why you deserve a nice, normal Suzy Homemaker type."

"You're wrong," Kevin said, jabbing a finger at her chest. "I'd get bored with a woman who doesn't own an axe and a shotgun."

"Really?"

"Yes, really. We can get couples' counseling. We can take quiet vacations. I don't care. But I know I want to spend the rest of my life with you, sweetheart."

Elsie smiled, showing her pearly white teeth, face radiating from forehead to neck. "I want to spend my life with you, too."

Kevin got down on one knee. He took one of her hands in his.

"Will you still marry me, Elsie?"

"I do. I love you!"

He stood up, and swept her in his arms, kissing her. The moment was sweet and tender, and Kevin wanted it to last forever.

Molly Biggins cleared her throat.

"Sweet of you two to figure out your problems," she said. "Do I need remind you of your other problems?"

The blood drained from Kevin's upper body, leaving him numb despite the euphoria he was feeling. His past was past, at least he won Elsie.

Elsie stepped in front of him, putting herself between him and Biggins.

"I know where Zack is staying," Elsie said. "If I lead you to him, will forgive Kevin's debt?"

Biggins chuckled. "Darling, I appreciate what you're doing. You'll be a fine wife for this man. But it's not that simple."

Kevin grabbed Elsie by the elbow. "Sweetie, it's okay. Not your problem."

She tugged away her arm. "Molly. You're a dominate lady, right?"

A wicked, serpentine smile glowed on Biggins' face. "I've demonstrated this already."

Gertrude groaned, but crossed her arms and said nothing.

Elsie smirked. "I know Zack's personal weakness. Do you want to know?"

Biggins gasped, and clutched her hands in front of her. "Well, perhaps."

"Forgive Kevin's debt, and I'll give you Zack's kryptonite."

"You push a hard bargain. Very well. But know this, if you disappoint me, I will make both your lives hard."

Elsie grabbed Biggins by the waist and leaned up to the tall blond woman. Biggins slouched down, putting her ear to Elsie's mouth. The serpentine smile grew wider.

Biggins kissed Elsie on the cheek.

"Well, well," said the Russian. "Nikolai, we have a long night ahead of us."

The big guy grunted, and shrugged his shoulders.

"Glad you like this," said Elsie. "I have a plan."

CHAPTER FIFTEEN

ELSIE KNOCKED ON ROOM 312. To her right was Kevin—now dressed in a clean white dress shirt with the sleeves rolled up and jeans—along with Mom and Brad, Kevin's best man. To her left was Molly, rubbing her hands like a praying mantis, and Nikolai, who held a green carpetbag and a video camera with a tripod.

She knocked again.

"Zaa-ack," she cooed. "It's me, Elsie. I've changed my mind. About us. Want to open up?"

She heard the bolt chain rattle on the other side, and the door open. Zack was in a pair of red-and-white striped boxer shorts and no shirt. He had a cute patch of chest hair that must have been trimmed, because it seemed to sweep down his stomach and pointed to his waist line.

"Hey doll," he said. "I knew you'd come around."

"May I come in?" Elsie said, tossing her hair to one side.

"Into my waiting arms, honey." Zack held out his arms, and made a smooching noise with his lips.

"Good." Elsie stepped into his embrace, her hands on his shoulders. Zack brought her in, arms around her waist. He massaged the small of her back.

Elsie leaned into Zack.

And squeezed his shoulder blades.

And then kneed him in the junk.

Hard.

Elsie's knee and thigh hurt, but in a satisfying way that made her smile.

Zack hunched over, groaning in falsetto with both hands cupped over the family jewels. She snatched him by the ear and dragged him deeper into his room.

He had a nice, cozy room with a king sized bed, a minibar with a fridge, and a widescreen TV that was currently playing a lesbian porno on mute.

Elsie wrangled him onto the bed. "Okay guys," she said. "Get in here!"

Kevin, Brad, Mom, Molly Biggins, and Nikolai crowded in. The place seemed awfully crowded suddenly. Kevin slammed the door shut, and clicked the chain in place. Molly yanked the window curtains closed.

"What the fuck?" Zack said. "Els, baby, if you wanted a gangbang, I could hook you up. Leave these creeps home next time!"

"Oh no, Zacky-poo," said Elsie. "It's time to get even."

"What do you mean, baby? I've always treated you with respect."

Nikolai tossed the carpetbag on the bed, and pulled out a long loop of silk rope.

Zack's eyes got round and huge right as the big Russian man grabbed him and hog-tied him.

"Well," said Elsie. "Zack, *baby*, I'd like to repay you. Honestly."

"This isn't right!" Zack squealed. "Damn you, bitch!"

"Aww," Elsie cupped his cheek, and lightly slapped him twice with her palm and backhand. "You're so cute!"

"This isn't over!" he yelled.

Molly Biggins grabbed him by back of the hair. She leaned into his ear, and said, "You're right, it's not."

Zack squirmed, trying to get away. But the knots Nikolai had made were too strong. Zack flopped around, like a fish out of water and made a break for the door.

He didn't get far.

Nikolai tackled him and threw him back on the bed. Then proceeded to tie Zack's right lower leg to his upper leg, and repeated the same with his left leg.

Elsie smirked, satisfied the king of douchebags wasn't going anywhere anytime soon.

"First order of business," she said. "Where is my gun?"

"Top left drawer, under the TV," said Zack. "Let me go now?"

Elsie opened the drawer, and sure enough was the Smith and Wessen 9mm.

"Come to mommy," said Elsie, cuddling the pistol in both hands and kissing it. "Did you miss me, too?"

"Fine, fine," Zack said, struggling and squirming against his bonds. "I'll give you a big kiss if you loosen me up."

Elsie pointed her precious gun at Zack's head. "Give me a reason not to shoot you, asshole."

Kevin clasped his hand on her wrist. "Honey, we agreed. No bloodshed before the wedding."

Elsie groaned. "Okay. But can I shoot his cell phone?"

Brad held up both hands and tip-toed to the nightstand, where Zack's phone was laying. "Wait, wait. That's what you brought me for, remember?"

"Don't look at those photos," said Elsie, with a playful smirk and a wink. She hoped Brad saw the wink. "Hate to shoot the best man."

He chuckled nervously as he played with the phone. "First, delete all the data. And then reset the system. And now..." Brad wiggled his fingers. "Abracadabra,

I've locked him out of his own phone. The photos are not only gone, he won't be taking more anytime soon."

"Aww man," said Zack. "You're a grade A douche, man."

"Thank you, Brad," Elsie said, putting her gun back in the holster it belonged to. "My last order of business is the black book."

Mom groaned, crossing her arms.

Zack laughed. "You know what's in the mysterious black book? Not what I expected, but hey, I had a little fun."

"Just tell me where it is," Elsie said.

"Can't I make a photocopy of it first?"

Mom slapped him across the face, hard enough to leave a handprint. "If the children weren't around," she said, "I'd kill you myself."

"Mother!" Elsie said. "He's an douchebag, but... Ah, never mind. Slap him again."

She did. The hit rang and echoed in the small hotel room.

"In the upper right drawer," mumbled Zack.

Elsie looked. Sure enough, sitting on top was a black, leather-bound book.

The cover had a title imprinted in gold-leaf lettering: *Molly's & Gertie's Black Book of Adventures.*

"Wait," Elsie picked up the book.

"No, honey," Mom said. "Don't!"

Too late. Curiosity and dread beat out common sense and curtesy. Elsie opened the black book to a random page. On each page were full-color photographs of Molly Biggins and Mom naked, in tantric poses.

"Oh," said Elsie. "Oh."

"Umm, oh," Kevin stuttered something non-sense. He grabbed the book out of Elsie's hands and slammed it shut. He handed it to Mom. "Guess this is yours, Mrs. Turner."

"Thanks, dear," Mom said, clutching the book to her chest. "And call me Gertrude, okay?"

"Your mother and I have a history together," said Biggins, a warm crooked smile breaking her icy countenance. "Going back to the mid-90s. God those were good years, da?"

"Yes, they were," Mom said, wistfully, wiping a tear from her eye. "We self-published this book. Cost a small fortune in those days."

"Da, but brings back some great memories."

"Mom," Elsie said. "Are you both crying?"

"No," she said, head down, and stepped over close to Biggins. "Here, Molly. You can have the black book. It was wrong of me to keep it from you."

Molly Biggins wrapped her arms around Mom and brought her in for a bear hug. "Thank you, Gertie. We have to catch up. After the wedding?"

"I'd like that." Mom returned the hug, and pecked Biggins on the cheek.

Kevin leaned over to Elsie's ear. "Are you crying, too?" he whispered.

"Oh shut up," Elsie smacked him on the chest.

"This is all sappy and shit," Zack yelled. "But I'm still here!"

"Darling," said Biggins. "We have not forgotten you."

"Time to go," said Mom. "Call me, Molly. There's a perfect tea shop downtown."

"I look forward to that," said Biggins. She reached into the carpetbag, looking at Zack. "As for you, I have a long night planned."

"Yawn," he said. "Just get it over with Sasquatch."

Elsie touched Biggins on the elbow. "You have my blessing to punish him any way you see fit."

Nikolai set up the tripod in one corner of the room, and gave a thumbs up.

"Oh we shall punish him," said Biggins. From the carpetbag, she pulled out an eight-inch strap-on dildo and a bottle of lube. "Russian style."

Zack's eyes nearly popped out of his head, as if he were already being anal fucked. He struggled against the ropes, thrashing, trying to get free. And going no-where.

"Elsie!" he yelled. "Els! Please, don't leave me! I'll—mmmmph!"

Nikolai stuck a red ball-gag into Zack's mouth and tied it behind his head.

"Much better, thank you Nikolai," said Biggins. "Hmm. Maybe we'll publish a red book for our new friend. Da?"

"Sounds like a bestseller," Mom said, sharing a giggle with Biggins.

"Bye asshole," Elsie patted Zack on the head. Then she hooked her arms in Kevin's and Brad's elbows. "Come on, boys. Let's get out of here before things get nasty."

When Mom closed the door behind them, Elsie could still hear Zack yelling through his ball-gag for help.

And still heard him from down the hall.

The elevator was thankfully quiet, except for the requisite elevator music. She pecked Brad on the cheek, making him blush.

And then she took Kevin in her arms and French kissed him.

EPILOGUE

ELSIE SHUT THE BRIDAL SUITE DOOR BEHIND HER, and leaned against it, sighing in sweet relief. Her white satin gown crushed against the door, but she didn't care. All the tension leading up to the wedding just sort of drifting out of her body, leaving her feeling euphoric and full of energy.

Kevin reached over her shoulder and slid the chain in place. "Mrs. Kincaid," he said.

"Hubby," she said.

His black tuxedo fit him perfectly. He looked like 007 with his bow-tie undone and collar button open, dashing and roguish, tied up in a neat packaging Elsie couldn't wait to unwrap. She reached around his waist, inside his jacket, and pulled Kevin closer.

He cupped her face in both hands and kissed her. His breath tasted of champagne and vanilla frosted wedding cake.

They had danced until midnight, which seemed to be the time when sleepy Wenakaga closed down for the night. There'd been the requisite speeches, the thank yous, the hugs and shaking hands. Then the guests all wanted to go back to their rooms.

Good thing, so did Elsie.

She heard a bed-frame squeaking repeatedly from directly below. In Zack's room. Hard to say, but she thought she heard muffled moaning as well.

Kevin shook his head, frowning. He heard it too. "Poor guy. I mean, I hated him. But he's going to be sore."

Elsie tore his tux jacket off. "So will you."

The ritual undressing took about thirty seconds. She popped the buttons off his shirt. He broke her dress's zipper. Then they were down to the underwear. She wore a black strapless bra and matching lace panties. He had on black silk boxers.

Elsie blinked and they were both naked, rolling around in bed and crinkling the sheets. Kevin rolled on top of her, the tip of his cock pressed to her lower lips.

"Baby, slow down," she said. For some stupid reason, her entire body felt wound up tighter than a stubborn wine cork that wouldn't pop. She was so nervous, her fingers shook. So she pressed them to Kevin's neck, hoping he wouldn't notice.

They'd had sex more times than she could count, including yesterday. How was this any different?

Kevin kissed her on the forehead, just a light touch with his lips. "You're right," he said. "This will be a long night."

"Won't I get my beauty rest?"

"That can wait for tomorrow."

"Good." Elsie pulled him for another kiss, on the lips. Which he gave her, then he grabbed her wrists and pinned her arms to the bed.

While he kissed down her neck.

To her shoulders. Breasts. Each nipple got a sweet kiss, sending ripples of pleasure through her body.

Kevin kept going lower. Down her stomach.

At her pelvis, he stopped, a wicked grin stretched across his face. Elsie exhaled, butterflies fluttering in her stomach, skin flushed and warm. She waited for him press his mouth on her sensitive pussy.

Instead, Kevin kissed and licked her thighs, skipping over her clitoris, barely touching the labia. Teasing with his tongue, back and forth, his moans growing wilder and louder with each passing.

Elsie grabbed him by the hair and pressed his face into her. He sank his tongue inside, nibbling at her, probing, making her squirm and buck for more.

He pressed a finger in, and curled his knuckles so he rubbed on her G-spot. Her pussy became wet, slick with both his saliva and her own moisture. Kevin didn't stop licking and sucking and finger-fucking, even when she wrapped her legs around his head. Not even when she bucked her hips at him.

The orgasm built little by little, the pressure so intense Elsie knew she'd explode if Kevin didn't let her come soon.

She white-knuckle clutched the bedsheets.

Sweat beaded on her brow, and down her back.

Her whole body shook and jittered with rapture.

Slick wet sounds, so satisfying, came from Kevin as he pounded his fingers in her pussy. Faster, quicker motions. Driving her crazy. And then...

Sweet release. The orgasm rocked her body from head to toes. Even then, Kevin didn't stop, only slowing slightly, mouth open to catch her squirt.

He kissed his way back up to her neck.

"I love you," said Elsie.

"Love you, too," Kevin said.

He gave her twenty-seven more orgasms before dawn.

And then they lived happily ever after.

THE "FUCKING" END

Creatures of Habit

THE PARLOR SMELLED OF LAVENDER flavored wax candles. Every table had at least one. Both end tables, as well as the coffee table with one giant candle ten inches in diameter. The curtains were wide open, but the outside was too dark for the afternoon.

Katie sat, back to me, at the piano. She was barefoot, in running shorts and a sports bra. A water bottle on the carpet, and pages of sheet music.

She was focused on the same two measures. I doubted she heard me come down the stairs. She woke me up early, on accident, by leaving the bathroom light on before slamming the screen door shut on her way to her daily mile run. I laid awake for a long time, listening to the thunderclaps and the gutters rattling in the windy violence. The storms rolled in later this morning, washed away yesterday's sticky humidity, and left more rain clouds.

Now the chaotic rumblings seemed far away, washed away by Katie's practice. A creature of habit, predictable as Sunday morning, beautiful as the steady *tap-tap* of notes she played. The only lights were her candles and the soft glow of the floor-lamp near the baby grand.

I stood in the double French doors, hands in pockets, watching Katie practice ragtime music. Sweaty hair clung to her bare shoulders, hiding her face. Her arms and legs were muscular and well toned. She had an lovely hourglass shape, one she worked at every day without fail, with curvy hips and a tight body.

I tiptoed into the kitchen and put on the coffee. The counters and cabinets were as organized as everything Katie did, all the way down to the magnets on the fridge and the three patterns in their own respective cupboards. She never simply threw something into a drawer. Everything had a place, or it didn't belong anywhere.

I managed complete silence, pouring the water slow and steady, betrayed only by the noisy coffee machine sputtering to life.

The music stopped. Katie—once a budding musician for a major orchestra—refused to practice with me in a twenty foot radius. As if I couldn't hear between the floorboards.

Soft, pitter-patter of bare feet on hardwood. The rustling of a robe being thrown on.

"Morning, Tom" she said.

"Hey you," I said, returning the warm smile. "Just in time for coffee."

"Good."

I poked my head into the fridge. Dozen eggs, butter, wheat bread, left-over lasagna from a night ago. Something was missing. I had no idea what.

When I turned around with the eggs in hand, Katie was staring at me, lips pressed tight and eyes narrow, hiding behind an empty coffee mug.

"The usual?" I said.

"Yes, please."

I prepared a much too large omelet with mushrooms, peppers, and bacon. She toasted bread. I tried hard to remember what my brain couldn't remember.

The more I thought, the fewer quality ideas came into my head. A little something I didn't notice, or forgot, or dismissed. For certain, Katie would quiz me on it later. Whatever "it" was.

"Penny for your thoughts," she said, leaning her body against mine as I stirred the eggs. Strong and skinny fingers pressed into my waist, massaging just below the elastic band.

"Might get a dozen thoughts for a penny," I said. "The way I'm going today."

"Oh?" Katie pressed her pelvis against me, hands slipping down my thighs. The spatula slipped from my grip. Hot breath tickled the back of my neck. "Is this helping?"

"Not at all."

My cock responded to her touching. The cotton fabric of my pajamas stretched. These eggs were going to waste. I desperately wanted her to reach into my pants and stroke me.

Instead, Katie kissed me on the neck. Her hands explored my back, my chest, twisting a nipple on the way to the shoulders.

The tingling in my body became a warm flush. The room unbearable hot. I turned off the stovetop. Only a cold shower would save me.

Eyes clenched shut. Breathing in ragged gasps as Katie massaged me.

I fought the urge to turn around. To take her. To force her to her knees.

That would end the sensations all too soon.

I had all morning. All day, actually.

"Do you want me to stop?" she whispered in my ear. Her tongue flitted across the lobe.

Words refused to form. So I shook my head.

I was in her control. In the way only she can control me.

Katie lifted my shirt. I pulled it the rest of the way off my head.

She pressed against me, warm skin on skin. My penis nearly popped the button on my pants.

Almost too much. I white-knuckle gripped the stove handle. She kissed me on the shoulder. Down the arm.

Fingers roaming. South.

Finding the drawstring. And finally pulling my pajamas down.

The full length of my cock popped out, at attention. The tip touched the warm metal of the stove.

"Please," I said.

"Eager, are we?"

"Yes. Please."

I stepped out of the pants. Naked and turned around in front of my wife.

Seemed unfair.

But I didn't want control.

I wanted to be fucked.

She slipped off her robe. The fabric rustled quietly when she tossed it aside.

Both her hands on my ass. One on each cheek.

"What do you desire?" she whispered into my ear.

"A blow job," I said. "A nasty. Sloppy blow."

Katie grasped my elbow and turned me around. A wicked smile colored her cheeks.

"Good," she cooed. "Thought you'd never ask."

A kiss on the lips. Pinch on both nipples.

The sports-bra came off. And tossed aside on top of the robe.

Both her nipples were erect. I touched them, softly, not quite pinching. Katie clutched my hands.

And went down on her knees.

She kissed the tip. Hands on my hips. She slid her wet tongue down my shaft.

I throbbed at the sensation. Eager for more.

A kiss at the base. Katie fondled my balls with lips and tongue. I gripped the edge of the stove, and tilted my head back.

Another lick, this time back up the shaft.

She swallowed me to the nub. My cock pierced the back of her throat. She breathed through her nose, slow, methodical. As if she were practicing yoga.

Katie's teeth scratched me as she released. Not enough to leave a mark. Enough to feel her loving bite.

Another pass. Her saliva dripped down my shaft, down my balls.

I bucked. My cock felt engorged. Ready to pop.

She wrapped fingers around the base and slapped my cock with her other hand.

"Be a good boy," she said.

I moved my lips. Words didn't come out.

Katie just laughed. A womanly chuckle.

She shook her head. Right before clamped her teeth down on me again.

This time, using both hands and mouth. One hand on my shaft. The other massaging my sack. The rhythm increased. Wet sucking and pumping. More desperate. I was certainly desperate. The pressure built up. More and more. Sweat dripped down my back. My heart rate increased. My breathing savage and ragged.

Katie squeezed and tugged my balls. Milking me for all I was worth.

I dipped into a haze full of the smell of my cock and her sweat.

My hips and legs went numb. My penis ached. Every muscle in my body tensed.

Until finally I exploded.

Just a squirt at first. And then a stream. Into her hair. On her face. Only a little made it into her mouth.

Katie kept sucking and scraping my cock.

Fluid dripped from her mouth to the floor. Cum or saliva, I couldn't tell in the moment.

She released me, and leaned back to admire her handiwork. My cock still throbbed, aching, ready for another round.

Katie got to her feet and kissed me. I tasted my own saltiness in her mouth.

"Be a dear and clean up," she said. "I might have more games for you later."

I smiled like a doofus as she walked away. The stairs creaked as she ran upstairs.

And like a flash of lightening as the most inappropriate time, I remembered what was missing from the fridge.

A bottle of Zinfandel I had bought yesterday. For Katie and me to share tonight.

It was gone. And I had no idea where it went to.

T W O

THE SHOWER TURNED ON UPSTAIRS after a few minutes. I spent the time thinking, over and over, *where the fuck is the wine?*

I opened the fridge again, scanned the counters and the island, looked under the sink. Nowhere. I had gone to the liquor store yesterday afternoon, bought the Zinfandel, and discussed politics with Benny the cashier.

And now I was losing my mind.

A peep out the patio door told me the wine wasn't likely outside. But I wasn't about to go out there yet, not in the buff, least of all while it was raining.

No way I could ask Katie where it went. Knowing her, she'd laugh and tease me about losing the wine until she told me what she did with it. Must be one of her silly games she played to frustrate me. She often hid things—toilet bowl cleaner, toothpaste, shaving cream—just to see if I noticed, and then send me on a quest to find the missing object.

I wiped my cum off the floor with hot water and a rag. The kitchen felt cold, now the sex was over.

So I staggered upstairs, still a bit shaky. The shower was still running, fog crept out the bathroom door like ghostly fingers. Inside was a sauna, oppressive and hot enough to peel the wallpaper.

The glass shower door concealed Katie as a feminine silhouette, washing her hair, hips rotating to and fro. After a while, she turned toward me, pressing a hand against the glass.

"Are coming?" she said. "Or just standing like a dope?"

"Out of come," I said. "Maybe I'll watch for a bit."

"Jack ass."

I slid open the shower door and stepped into the sticky hot spray. The water burned my skin. I had no chance to get used to the temperature, because Katie grabbed me by the back of the hair, fingers curled tight, and kissed me. Breathing suddenly became hard in the steamy shower with our tongues locked together.

To my surprise and pleasure, I sprang back to attention, my cock head touching Katie's abs, just below her breasts.

I grabbed her arms, above the elbows, and wrestled her away.

"Is something in the water?" I said.

"What do you mean?"

"I mean, you're insatiable today."

"Only today?"

Katie bent her knees, about to go down on me again. But I stopped her with my fingers under her chin. I pecked her lips again, and then got down on my knees.

I spread her thighs apart, and planted little kisses on the inside of her legs. Up. Closer to the spot.

And skipped over to the thin landing strip above and grabbed her ass in both hands. Katie's eyes slitted, like a hypnotized viper. One wrong move, and she'd attack. So I let my hands keep her hypnotized. Wandering up her hips and waist, following the curves, the smooth wet skin, the underside of her breasts.

A moan escaped her mouth.

I brushed my mouth against her pink folds. The pussy musk was already heavy. No amount of soap and water could clean that.

A little taste, wet and sweet. I nibbled her clit, slow and gentle. A lick here with a rough tongue. Some pressure there with my lips and teeth. Across the opening, around the labia, and pulling it apart like a flower, little by little.

Until finally...

I slid my middle finger in. Just the first knuckle. Enough to make her squirm her hips. I pulled back out, but not quite a full retreat, and flicked her clit. Pressing, faster, round and round.

Katie tossed her head back, lolling side to side, lost in the rhythm. Her breasts jiggled when she bounced on my finger. I responded by shoving more into her pussy.

Two fingers.

Faster. Wet, slick sounds with each pump.

Her moans became desperate. Needy.

She tried to say something. Mumbles really. Dirty talk. "Fucker" maybe. Or "fuck yes don't stop fuck fuck fuck..."

Hard to tell, when she lost control.

Katie grasped me by the hair and shoved my face to her pussy. So I could worship her better.

I lapped at her bean, and pumped her with my fingers.

"I need... need," she said. "Your cock. Please."

My answer was to keep eating her.

To keep sliding in and out. Fast enough to make my arm sore.

Katie quivered. She pushed my head away now. Completely lost.

She rubbed her clit while I finger fucked her hole.

Warm juice dripped down my forearm.

Katie leaned against the shower wall, now spent and exhausted. I got back to my feet and kissed her. No tongues this time. Just a gentle lip lock.

"You'll get my cock," I said. "Later. If you're good."

"Oh God." Katie nestled into my shoulder and I held her close under the shower spray.

THREE

THE RAIN CLOUDS FINALLY PARTED. Sunshine poured into the parlor window in streams across the baby grand. Turned out to be a nice day after all.

This was our routine on the weekend. Wake up. Do our own activities. Fuck each other senseless. Then ignore one another until dusk.

Katie dressed and left with purse in one hand and a list in the other. "Gone shopping," was all she said.

I wore a t-shirt, jeans, and sandals. I had a mission while she was gone. By damn, that bottle of wine stood no chance against my persistence. We were sipping Zinfandel tonight.

The patio was clear. The smells of spring were in the air—tulips and roses in the garden, fresh cut grass next door, new buds on the trees. No wine. Nothing but the outdoor furniture, the sun umbrella, and wet cedar.

But on second glance, a glint caught my attention. Between the lounge chairs, on the deck. A fluted glass.

With pale pink lipstick smeared on it. Katie wore red, unless it was a blue day.

I picked up the glass, unsure what to think yet. I didn't know of any friends who wore that shade.

The doorbell rang. Twice in a row. I nearly dropped the flute. Instead I placed it in the kitchen sink. On the way to the door, I wondered whether to wash off the lipstick smear or not.

My mind wandered to a situation where Katie accused me of having female company over. But that was absurd. We had talked about swinging, but that was all it was. And our sexual energy was always spent on each other to the point of near exhaustion at the end of Sunday.

I unlocked the deadbolt and opened the door to a gorgeous and skimpily dressed woman. She was younger than Katie, no older than thirty. A pair of wedge sandals accentuated her calf and thigh muscles. The hip pockets poked out of the bottom of her cut-off denims. A black tank top clung to her torso. Her hair was blue-black, and fell lazily about her shoulders, which made her green eyes all the more exotic.

"Hello," I said. "Can I help you?"

The woman shrugged, a blush darkening her skin from the cleavage busting out her top, to her neck, up to her cheeks. Her top rose with her shoulders, showing off a slice of her midriff. She promptly pulled her shirt back down tight.

"Tom?" she said. "Katie's husband."

"That's what she calls me. You a friend of hers?"

"Yeah, we work together. Well, used to. I've moved to another company."

"Want to come in?"

She nodded quickly, and stepped inside. She smelled like a bottle of lavender lotion, the kind Katie likes so damned much.

"Sorry. I didn't catch your name."

"Mandy." The smile pinched her dimples deep.

"Something to drink? I have soda, water, maybe wine somewhere."

"I'd love a Zinfandel, if you have some."

"Might be fresh out."

"Shucks!"

"But I'll look."

"Thank you."

I made a show of poking my head into the fridge. I shrugged and raised my hands in mock defeat. "Beer, instead?"

"Naw. Too early to drink. I'd love some raspberry flavored water, though."

"You seem to know my fridge better than me." I poured her a tall glass of the water, and myself one too.

"I've been over before," Mandy said. We clinked glasses in toast. "Thanks."

"What'd you say your name was?"

She repeated it for me. I nodded sagely, as if trying to burn the name into my memory. She seemed familiar now, not that I'd met her, more like Katie had mentioned her once or twice.

Mandy stared at me as she drank, eyes narrow, cute smile dancing across her face, a little secret caught up in her eyebrows. She was cute, and almost naked if not for the skimpy clothes.

For some dumb reason, my cock decided it liked Mandy a bit too much. I pressed my pelvis into the kitchen island to keep it from being too obvious.

In a flash, my mind wandered to the fantasy of having two woman in my kitchen, within a twenty-four hour span.

Then I banished the thought.

My dick hurt with the awkward angle I had jabbed it into against the island.

"Not sure when the woman will be back," I said.

"Huh? Oh!" Mandy laughed like a hyena, too high-pitched. Might've been annoying if I weren't undressing her with my mind. "It's fine. I can come back later."

"You're no bother."

Mandy set her glass down. Her eyes turned a shade serious. "No. I think I'll come back around later. I'll give Katie a ring this afternoon."

"Sounds like a plan." I tried to make my smile winsome. Not sure if my disappointment helped.

I walked Mandy to the door. At the last moment, she turned. A little too close to me, one boob pressed against my forearm. The blush in her cheeks returned, rosier, and migrated to her forehead.

"I hope to see you again," she said.

"You're welcome her anytime," I said. "Come back soon."

"Oh," she said. "I will."

I opened the door for her, and Mandy left. She strutted down the driveway, to a shiny red car, not even turning around to wave goodbye.

My cock made a tentpole for the whole neighborhood to see.

FOUR

I TRIED TO WATCH TV, but it was too hard. Literally.

Channel surfing only brought up shows that bored me, so my brain wandered from infomercials and badly scripted soap operas to... sex scenes between my wife and Mandy.

"Perv," I said out loud. Did no good. My cock plugged its ears with cotton swabs, and if I stayed around the house for ten more minutes, there was going to be cum flushed down the toilet.

Katie would be disappointed.

So I turned off the tube and grabbed the keys. The first bottle of wine was lost to the great beyond, apparently where alcohol went to die, undrunk and lonely. I hope they have good beer on tap there.

The only option now was to just buy a new wine.

I drove to the liquor store, focusing on traffic and thinking about pink elephants the entire time so Mandy had no chance of making me hard.

The Third Street Liquors was on Michigan Avenue, for reasons Benny never fully explained to me. It was located conveniently next to an insurance man, and beneath a real estate office.

Inside always smelled like a tin can sprayed with lemon scented air freshener. Benny, a white haired man with a serpent tattoo crawling up one arm, stood guard at the cash register.

"Here to claim the Doll?" he crooned, a wizened crooked smile twisting unnaturally.

"You done with her?" I said.

"Pretty girls like that don't give me the time of day. Unless I blindfold 'em first."

"Now I know what to look forward to."

Benny pointed towards the wine section, nodding and chuckling.

I found Katie, slowly walking down the aisle, a finger on a Zinfandel. I hated watching her shop. Always the same brand, but she had to find the *one* bottle.

"Hey, Doll." I grabbed her from behind by both elbows.

Katie jumped, jabbing me in the ribs.

"Careful, mister," she said. "Good thing I know what you smell like."

"Otherwise?"

"You'd get a major ass kicking."

"I'd deserve it too."

"Yeah, for sure." She walked away from me, pretending to look at other wines. "So? What brings you here, stranger?"

"Thought I'd pick up a Merlot."

"Good God, why? You know how reds don't agree with me."

"All too well. Which means more for me."

"Then buy a Zinfandel while you're at it."

"You used to like Chardonnays. How about we shake things up."

"I don't want to shake. Just buy what I want."

"We could go all out and get champagne."

"Hmm. I'd like that. But good idea to have zinfandel on hand too."

"What if I only brought cash enough for one bottle?"

"You have a credit card, don't you?"

"Maybe."

"What the hell does that mean? Have you been drinking already?"

"Want to smell my breath?"

"Nope."

"Shucks. So one merlot. One champagne. One... what did you want?"

I think Katie's eye roll displaced a tidal wave somewhere.

Hiding my goofy grin best I could, I picked up a zinfandel and a merlot, even though I didn't really want the latter.

"Funny thing," I said. "Seems like I bought wine yesterday. Wonder what became of that one?"

Katie pressed her lips tight in a straight line, her cheeks flushing rosy. "Haven't the foggiest."

"Maybe I'm just losing my mind," I said.

"Must be the problem."

I stared at her long and hard (definitely hard, Katie tells me long too). Her tight lips relaxed, showing a hint of white teeth, pink gums, the flush turning joyful. She laughed.

Katie pressed a hand against my chest. "Be a good boy," she said. "Put those wines in the fridge and I'll bring home a surprise."

"Really?"

"Yup." Her hand slid down lower, to the belt line.

"What is it?" I whispered.

"You'll like... it," she said. "I hope."

"I like everything you do," I said. "Except for vacuuming. That's kind of annoying."

Katie slapped me on the chest.

I winked, kissed her goodbye, and smacked her on the ass before pulling away. I mouthed the words "I love you", watched her do the same, and I walked away.

A million ideas sprang to mind about her secret surprise. One idea in particular excited me the most, but I knew I shouldn't hope for it.

Mandy.

FIVE

I MEANT TO TAKE A NAP THAT AFTERNOON. Didn't happen. Instead, I watched TV, checked email, read the sports page, and played solitaire too many times to count.

Finally, at six in the evening, Katie pulled into the garage and honked the horn. When I met her, she kicked the back door closed with her foot, planted a kiss on my lips and shoved two bulky grocery bags into my arms.

"Hmm, groceries," I said. "What a wonderful surprise."

She lightly smacked me on the cheek. "Put those away. The surprise is still in the car."

"You're killing me."

"That's the plan."

We turned away from each other, I headed to the kitchen, she to the garage. I managed a sneak peak over my shoulder, but all I could see before she slammed the door shut again was the hood of the car and Katie's self-assured Cheshire grin.

I set the bags down on the counter, much to the relief of my shoulder muscles. I took a look inside. Spaghetti, tomato sauce, eggs, fresh fruit. Some of the makings for dinner and breakfast. We weren't going out anytime soon.

I sped-walked back to the door and got there in time to see Katie with one hand extended out for the knob.

"Get the rest," she said, a full grin this time.

"Yes, ma'am."

I stepped out to the garage. Somebody sat in the passenger seat of Katie's car. Somebody with blue-black hair and a cute face. I opened the car door. She held a bottle of zinfandel in her lap.

"Mandy?" I hoped my voice didn't sound too hope-ful. Too pleading.

"Tom," she said. "I was about to run away if you took much longer."

"I like to be timely." I extended a hand to help her out of the car. "One of my better qualities."

"So I've heard." Mandy's palm was warm to the touch, sweaty, and smooth like a piece of silk. I liked her touch already.

"What else have you heard?"

"Much."

"Like wine? To drink?"

"Much," she repeated. "I... uh, drank your bottle last night. Me and Katie."

"Figures. Now we'll all have to drink even more."

"I could use a drink."

"Me too, I think."

I picked up the rest of the groceries from the backseat, and led Mandy into the house. She smelled wonderful, like a girl-scented breeze that found its way into my home. Her hips swayed with each step, back straight, lean calf muscles stretching and knotting, the wedge sandals clip-clopping on the hardwood floor. Mandy glanced here and there, as if seeing the room for the first time. Probably wasn't, if she had secretly been here last night.

In the kitchen, Katie already had the perishables put away and three wine glasses set out on the island. I poured.

"So," I said. "How long have you ladies been planning this?"

"Too long," said Katie. "I could barely keep quiet anymore."

"We had something of a wager," said Mandy. "I lost."

"Oh?" I said.

"She didn't think I could run a mile every morning for a month," said Katie.

"Sounds like a real supportive friend."

"It's not like that," said Mandy, hiding behind her glass, one hand reached out as if to slap me. She held back, uncertainty in her eyes.

"What was the nature of this wager?"

"Since I'd broken up with my fiancee, we'd talked a lot. About things. Girl chat. And..."

"And one night," said Katie, "she was too intoxicated for her own good. But at least I got her to write it down."

Mandy blushed a deep shade of crimson as she poked around in her handbag, finally pulling out a piece of folded up loose leaf paper. She handed it to me, as if passing a dirty note during school.

Pink penned handwriting scrawled across the paper:

I, Mandy, do hereby declare that if my bestest friend, Kaite, can run one (1) mile every morning for one (1) month, I will suck off her husband until she is satisfied. XOXO Mandy. P.S. I will do much more than suck him off.

The first question that came to mind was: *Were you rooting for Katie to win?* But I closed my mouth before I could say that. Instead I took a sip of wine.

Every man's dream, come true for me right here in my home. Two women in bed. This had never happened to me. Sure, Katie and I talked about swinging, but I kept no illusions. I very much wanted to fuck both my wife and her best friend, tonight, because such an opportunity doesn't happen more than once. By the cheery, wide-eyed, goofy grinned look Katie was giving; I had my wife's blessing.

"Do you approve?" she said.

"Yes. Very much." I pulled Katie into my arms and kissed her. A light touching of lips, meeting of tongues, and I pushed her away.

Mandy glanced away, wine glass in hand as if she were a bored patron at a boring art gallery party, blush coloring her tanned skin.

I took her hand. "You're welcome to bow out of this. We won't tell anyone. And we won't bring it up again."

"Thank you," she said. "But I've come this far."

"You sure."

Mandy nodded, her hair bobbing with the motion. "I've been thinking about you since Katie first showed me your photo."

I pulled her closer. "I hope it was a face shot. Maybe the one with the brown shirt?"

My wife slapped me on the shoulder. "Don't be an idiot."

Mandy took a step forward, eyes roving up and down my body. I clenched her around the waist and drew her in the rest of the way. She kissed me. Tentatively, at first, a fast exploration to see what would happen.

I gave her a slip of my tongue. It'd been so long since I'd done this with another woman, other than Katie. I wasn't entirely sure what to do next. Mandy wrapped her arms over my shoulders, and grabbed a fistful of my hair. I liked where this was going. We locked tongues. I pushed her hard against me, pressing her onto my manhood.

Mandy tilted her head back and giggled. "I can't believe this is happening!"

"Last chance to say no." I was surprised at how husky—how growly—my voice was.

She took a sip of wine and set the glass aside. Katie had her backside leaned against the kitchen sink, staring at us, mischievous grin playing at the corners of her mouth.

"One word," said Mandy, leaning close again, her breasts squashed into my torso. "Yes. Just yes."

I grabbed her by the elbows and turned her around, pushing her into the island. A wild expression came over her face, eyes wide, mouth parted enough to see white teeth, nostrils flared. We brushed lips.

I massaged her waist. Her hips. Back up, gently cupping each breast. The kissing became harder, wetter, passionate, like suffocating but more pleasant. I slid one hand back downward, and parted her thighs, the soft skin contrasting with the rough denim of her shorts.

And pressed my middle finger on top of the sweet spot, rubbing. A primal moan escaped Mandy's throat, which made me press hard and faster. I couldn't wait to get those shorts off, could imagine the smell of her pussy, but I didn't want to stop kissing her.

She pushed me away, arm's length, her breathing savage, bosom heaving.

"I... need..." she said. "Need to pay my wager."

I cupped her face in both hands. "Upstairs in the bedroom. Pay it in full."

Mandy reached up and kissed me once more. I took her by the hand, and my wife in the other hand, and led them upstairs.

Now I was sort of clear headed, I was entirely uncertain if I could keep up tonight.

S I X

BY THE TIME WE REACHED THE BEDROOM, Katie already had her top off and her shorts unzipped, and left her clothes in a trail. All that remained was black lacy lingerie and an ankle bracelet.

The bedroom was dark with the curtains pulled tight. Had I known about the company, I'd have left the floor lamp on. Instead, I reached into the darkness, felt around along the wall, and nearly knocked the lamp down trying to find it.

The light was enough to see with, not enough to read in. The king size bed was made, covers and a quilt pulled up tight underneath three pillows. The duvet wasn't put on, nor were the decorative pillows Katie liked.

She meant business tonight.

Katie and I pulled the covers down, exposing the satin sheets underneath. Mandy leaned against the door, watching us.

"You can't chicken out on me now," said Katie. She grasped Mandy by the hands and yanked her friend into the room.

"I'm not chickening out," said Mandy. "I'm assessing the situation."

"For what?"

"Predators, maybe."

"Girl, we're the predators here."

The women approached me, slow as if in a bad horror movie where the monster can't run for some unexplained reason. My heart pounded, thudding in my chest and throat and head.

Watching the women circle me, like a pack of wolves coming in for the kill.

Both sets of eyes roamed up and down. Devouring me.

Katie yanked off my belt. In a second my pants were undone.

Mandy held back. A moment longer.

I pulled her into my arms.

Right as Katie pulled my pants down, along with my boxers.

I sprang to attention in a semi-limp way.

The girl in my arms pulled at my shirt. I helped her take it off all the way.

My wife's warm lips nibbled on my cock.

I kissed Mandy. Slow. A taste.

A moan escaped from deep in her throat. I could tell nobody had touched her in too long. I slid my fingers up her side.

And cupped one breast.

She didn't seem to mind one bit.

The kissing became needy.

Then desperate.

Katie swallowed me. Scrapping her teeth along my shaft.

Bringing me closer to the edge without going too far.

The two women each a different rhythm.

One swallowed me whole and spat me back out. Over and over.

The other danced along the surface. Lips and tongue mingling, but not committing. Teasing without entirely meaning to.

I leaned my backside against the mattress. The dissonant rhythms passed through my body, down to the core. A painful pleasure that unsettled as it soothed.

Mandy pushed away from me. She panted. Eyes slitted, watching.

I grabbed her by the hair and nudged the woman to her knees. She didn't resist.

Katie offered her my cock. I had no choice in the matter. My pleasure, and my orgasm, was out of my control. At least I was familiar with my wife's touch. The way she licked, her patterns and preferences.

But this stranger was a wild card.

My heart-rate skyrocketed. My brain flooded with hormones. I twitched as Mandy wrapped her mouth around me. She swallowed me to the hilt and gagged. Only needed a second to catch her breath again and relax.

And then they played tennis with my cock. One sucked the head, the other licked the balls. They took turns. One after the other. Slurping, gagging, sighing.

Somewhere in that, Mandy took off her shirt and bra. She took control. Not quite pushing Katie out of the way, but taking longer and faster passes on me.

My wife sat back on her heels, watching. She held my hand while her friend blew me. Mandy now used both her mouth and one hand.

Up, down. Eyes closed.

Harder. More violent.

I was so close. I could feel it in my balls, rising to the tip, even gushing a little.

I clutched Mandy's wrist and grabbed a fistful of her hair. I had to make her stop.

She almost didn't. I pushed her away. So close.

Mandy panted. Skin flushed, sweaty at the temples. She squeezed one of my thighs. Her smile was too cute for words.

I patted the mattress. "Question of the night is, which one of you goes first?"

"The guest, of course," said Katie, winking. Who the wink was for, I wasn't entirely sure.

"Top or bottom?" I said.

"Bottom," said Mandy. I motioned for her to lay down. Instead she pressed her fingers into my biceps. On her tip-toes, she kissed me. "You on the bottom."

"Yes ma'am."

I rolled over and laid on my back. My body was wired, as if on a caffiene high but much, much better. I shook at the knees and elbows in anticipation.

Mandy grabbed my cock in one fist and straddled me. The motion was rough. She rubbed her clit for a few seconds. I throbbed painfully. Came close to begging.

Her pussy was already wet. Glistening.

Finally Mandy impaled herself on me. Katie was at my neck, kissing my collarbone and pinning one of my arms down.

With my free hand, I clutched the bedsheets tight.

Mandy started slow. Sliding up and down. One finger on her clit. Pinching a pink nipple with the other hand.

Then faster. Rougher. Bouncing. Skin slapping on skin.

My wife's kisses became more intense. As if the women were working in tandem.

They were.

And I was a piece of meat. Ready to blow.

But Mandy slowed down. Almost stopping.

I moaned and writhed under her. I bucked under her.

She didn't respond. Just sat on me, like a queen on top of a horse. Eyes slitted. Lips parted.

Mandy pressed a hand to my stomach and shoved her hips roughly against me. Downward. I stopped bucking.

I had no control. She knew it too.

She gyrated her hips. The pressure on my cock increased.

Katie's kisses went south, to my nipples. She grabbed a fistful of my hair, as if to hold my head in place. To make me look at this beautiful woman fucking me with no mercy.

Mandy had me balls deep. I still didn't entirely believe what was happening.

The pounding increased. Her pussy dripped all over my member. The smell of two pussies—similiar but distinct—filled my head.

Making me dizzy.

Faster yet. Mandy made desperate animal noises.

Two hands on my chest now. Katie's lips and tongue found my ear lobes.

Slap. Slap. Slap.

Faster.

The bed squeaked.

I felt it. The first glow just above my balls.

"Oh God. Oh fuck. Fuck."

I couldn't hold back much longer.

Mandy doubled her effort. Grinding on me. Pumping me.

"I'm gonna... Stop. Please. Please."

Mandy released me from her pussy with a wet plop. Out of the hole, back into her hand.

She stroked me. Didn't take much.

I exploded in her touch. A jet of semen sprayed her in the face.

The rest of it landed on my stomach. Katie was nice enough to clean up after me with her tongue.

All of us continued to make out, but at a much slower pace. I kissed both women, passionately, and played with both of their pussies.

Mandy passed out first. I followed not longer after. I remember Katie being on my right, Mandy on the left.

Close to noon the next day, I heard the front door slam. Mandy was still in my arms, snoring. I dozed off again.

Later, I awoke. Mandy had shifted, and lightly played with my morning wood. I had no idea if she was awake or not.

Piano   music   drifted   from   downstairs.

Gone to the Dogs

ONE

THE MAN ROUNDED THE CORNER, like clock-work. Every evening at seven o'clock, he walked his black pug in front of Kacy's bungalow, her little piece of heaven.

At first, she stared at him through the sheer curtains of her front dining room window. He nearly always wore cargo shorts, a plaid short sleeve shirt, tucked in of course, and sandals. At least he didn't wear socks. The way he walked—strolled—through the subdivision, head slightly down, each step the same stride, keeping pace with his old dog... that's what intrigued Kacy.

He was reasonably tall, sure. And handsome in a rugged fashion. Not so dark, with mousy brown hair and freckles. But he strolled as if he didn't care what anyone thought of his plaid shirt and pet pug.

After a week or so of staring at him from inside like a creepster, Kacy made it a point to water her bushes when he walked past.

As the summer grew hotter, she switched from jeans to skimpy shorts and t-shirts to form fitting tank tops. As her clothing choices got smaller, the more sideways his glances at her became. He always smiled nicely with big bright teeth, and said hello, but never glanced backwards when he walked away.

Tonight, she wore a black and gold bikini and flip-flops.

The humidity clung to her skin like a gauzy fabric. She made sure to have her back to him, watering hose in one hand, and screwed on the spray attachment. She bent over to pull a weed from her bush.

Kacy blew a string of hair out of her face, her breath minty fresh. She had brushed her teeth not long ago.

The pug snorted and wheezed. Kacy turned her head, and saw the man staring point blank at her back-side. He blushed enough to hide his freckles and picked up his pace.

"Hey, dude," said Kacy.

"Yes, neighbor?" he said. The pug pulled at the leash, anxious to be going. And then flopped down on the grass.

"What do you think you're gawking at?"

"I'm... sorry. I'll just be leaving."

"No. I want to know. What were you staring at?"

He shrugged. "It's nothing. Sorry."

"Stop saying sorry or I'm going to spray you." Kacy lifted the hose, to make her point. She squeezed the trigger once, a thin jet of water gushed out.

The man held up his free hand. "Whoa. Truce?"

"Tell me your name."

"To report me to the police? No way."

"Maybe." This time, Kacy shrugged. "I just want to know your name. You've walked by here enough. Can't we be neighbors?"

"Sure."

"Assuming we are neighbors. And you're not some creepy stalker and your van is parked around the corner."

"Every stalker needs a sidekick," he pointed to his now snoring pug. "Mine happens to be old and cranky."

"Cute dog," said Kacy. "Mind if I pet him."

"Her. Her name's Gertie."

"Hey there, Gertie." Kacy knelt down and stroked the pug's grey and wrinkled forehead. The dog opened her eyes, snorted, and raised her head. "Who's a good doggie?"

Gertie sniffed Kacy's hand and laid her head back down.

The man shifted his weight from foot to foot. He looked everywhere but at Kacy. She wasn't entirely sure if his face was red from the heat, or for some other reason.

"So," he said at last. "What's your name?"

"Excuse me?" she said.

"Just wanted to know your name."

"I asked you first. Only fair."

"I'm at a loss."

"Start talking," Kacy held up the hose and took aim. "Or things will get nasty."

"You just want to get me wet," he said.

"Maybe."

"I'm sorry, but..."

Kacy squeezed the trigger to half force and sprayed the guy in his chest. His plaid shirt turned a darker blue in two seconds. Gertie raised her head, letting out a grouchy bark.

"Jesus, lady!" he said.

"Is your name Jesus?" Kacy dropped the watering hose aside.

"No. But close."

"Joshua?"

"Give the woman a prize."

"I should spray you again for being snarky."

"You'd like that."

Kacy stood up. "Maybe."

"That your favorite word?"

"Maybe."

"We're at an impasse."

"How so?"

"Two choices," said Joshua. "Either I can walk away and never walk my dog down this street again."

Kacy didn't like that choice. A lump formed in her throat. She hoped she hadn't pushed Joshua away before getting to know him. She tossed the water hose aside and held her hands out in mock surrender.

"Option number two?" Kacy said.

"You invite me in for a nightcap," he said.

"Oh. Uh..." She was thrown off guard. This scenario hadn't occurred to her when she daydreamed about this guy.

Sure, she wore a bikini to get his attention. Now she had it, Kacy wasn't sure she wanted it. And what if he really did have a van parked around the corner?

What if he was just a nice guy?

"Look," Joshua said. "That was a lame come on. I'm sorry."

Kacy bent over, making sure he saw the length of her thigh, and picked up the watering hose again.

"What did I say about the word sorry?" she said.

"Not to say it? Sorry."

She sprayed him again. Lower this time, at the stomach. Rivulets dripped from his shirt to his shorts. He laughed. A hearty, good natured chuckled that started from his diaphragm. Kacy clasped a hand over her mouth, stifling her reaction, and ended up joining him anyway.

She told him her name.

"Come on," Kacy said. "I'll hang your shirt on my laundry line. So it'll dry, of course."

Joshua tugged at his collar. "You sure about this?"

Kacy turned away and headed toward the front door. She glanced back over one shoulder, tucking her hair over an ear.

"Hurry up," she said. "Before I change my mind."

T W O

SHE HUNG THE SHIRT ON THE LINE OUTSIDE her patio door. Now the mystery man—Josh—sat on her sofa, bare-chested and barefoot. He had a finely toned body, not exactly chiseled, but well formed with flat abs and nicely shaped muscles.

A shame to cover that with plaid.

The pug had already fallen asleep on the floor, in front of Kacy's TV, already snoring like a twenty pound freight train.

She brought in two shot glasses and a bottle of whiskey, the one from Gina's bachelorette party a year ago. The bottle had sat unopened in Kacy's cupboard the whole time.

He smelled clean, like he'd just gotten out of the shower and thrown on some aftershave.

"Is this how you normally pick up guys?" he said.

"Naw," Kacy poured drinks. "Thought I'd try something new. See where it went."

"Where is it going?"

She handed him one of the shots.

"I don't know," she said. "It's kind of early for a nightcap."

"Cheers."

"Cheerio. Then."

They clinked glasses and drank. She tilted her head back, watching him from the corner of her eyes. Kacy suspected he was doing the same.

She finished first. The alcohol burned all the way down. Kacy's head twitched a little. He sipped his whiskey, and then tossed the rest down the hatch.

And coughed.

His entire body spasmed, head jerking, shoulders hunched.

"You okay, sweetie?" said Kacy.

"Wow," he said. "Some poison."

"You wanted a nightcap." She filled his glass with another dose.

"To bad decision making." Josh raised his glass.

"Bad decisions." She clinked glasses with him and they drank again.

He tried to hide his reaction. He tilted his head, squeezing his eyes shut. It only had the effect of making him blush.

Kacy found it cute.

They sat on the couch, heads twitching. He coughed.

"Hate to say it," Josh said. "But I'm buzzed."

"Yeah," said Kacy. "Now we're properly inebr... inebria... fuck it."

"Intox..." he said. "Intoxic..."

"Drunk and disorderly!"

"Hell yes!"

The pug raised her head. Her glassy eyes seemed to say, *fuck you humans, keep it down, some of us are sleeping.*

Josh's smile was loose and playful. Kacy couldn't help but look down, below his neckline. She wasn't drunk yet. Just enough to feel tipsy.

That scared her and excited her at the same time. Like being in school again, uncertain of what to do, how to do it. Had it really been that long since her last fuck buddy?

"You okay?" said Josh.

"No," said Kacy. "Yes."

"Way to send mixed signals."

"Sorry." She took his glass away and set it on the coffee table.

"Do I need to spray you?" said Josh. "With a watering hose. Totally what I meant."

She looked at him, checking her out. His eyes were soft and brown. Kind eyes. If a wee bit drunk and scattered at the moment.

Josh moved, shifting his weight away from her. As if to stand. Kacy placed a hand on his wrist. His skin was warm to the touch. Smooth. Even the hair was smooth.

And it just felt good to touch a man.

To control him. To make him stay when she didn't want him to leave.

Kacy leaned forward. Eyes half closed.

He didn't pull away. The smell of his skin and hair was crisp.

Closer. Lips nearly touching.

Josh cupped her elbows. A strong grasp, barely touching her. Pulling her in a tad closer.

She adjusted her hips.

He cleared his throat. And straightened his shoulders.

Kacy opened her eyes. Wondering why she was touching noses with him.

And then he kissed her.

Lips spreading lips. Tongues probing. A moan escaped. Sounded feminine. Must've come from her throat.

Kacy pulled away. Hands flat on his chest. Her breathing was ragged.

"No mixed signals there," said Josh.

"Bad decisions and all," she said.

"You sure about this?"

"You keep asking that."

Kacy grabbed the back of his head by the hair. She pushed him down, into the couch.

And kissed him.

She straddled him, wiggling her hips against his bulging shorts. His mouth tasted hot, like a sultry day. Kacy wondered what the rest of him tasted like. She decided she wasn't waiting too long to find out.

But she could take her time on the couch.

THREE

SHE STOOD UP ONCE, PRESSING a palm firmly into his chest to make sure he knew to stay, and closed the curtains. Now the late evening sun was tinged red and came in a hazy line through the curtain gaps. The dog still snored on the carpet, but Kacy found it easy to ignore that. She was lost in Josh's scent and touch. The way he grabbed her hips and bucked against her every so often, strong fingers pressed into her skin.

Her body felt hot to the core, and she was fairly certain the air conditioning worked fine. Sweat beaded down her arms and legs. Underneath her, Josh burned

up as well. His fingers wandered up her body, slow, methodical, touching her hips and waist in massaging circles.

Higher up still.

All the way up her spine. He massaged her shoulder
blades, pulling her closer to his hot body. In a smooth
motion, he untied her bikini top.

Kacy yanked it away, her breasts bared to him completely. She couldn't believe this was happening. Too
many nights she put herself to sleep with a battery
powered toy, imagining a situation like this. Now half
naked—no, near naked—in front of a man she'd been
fantasizing about for some time. None of her day-
dreams involved a pug snoring five feet away, but beg-
gars aren't choosers. And Kacy wasn't a beggar.

She grabbed a clump of his hair and leaned into his
ear.

"Come upstairs," she whispered. "If you want to see
more."

The playful ear to ear grin on his face was precious.
Kacy tossed her bikini top at him, right over his eyes,
and rolled off. Her inner thighs already burned from
pinning him down for so long.

She turned away, but didn't get very far.

Josh smacked her across the ass. He wrapped both
hands around her waist, pinching in the delicate area,
and pulled her back to his lap.

Kacy fell across him haphazardly.

He braced her neck and back in his strong arms.

"I'm a terrible listener," he said. "What were you saying about upstairs?"

"At least you admit it," Kacy said.

"Huh?"

She smacked him on the cheek. Hard enough to make a sound. Not enough to leave a handprint.

A love slap.

She stood, pushing off his chest and thigh. Unsteady on her feet. She didn't turn around, trusting him to follow.

Josh put his hand in hers.

She led him up the stairs. Around the corner. Into the dark bedroom. Kacy told him to wait at the door, while she went to the night table and flicked on a light.

He didn't wait very long.

The lamp light illuminated his face. The bedroom was mellow, dark enough to see. Josh wrapped an arm around her waist.

His other hand glided up her torso. Cupping her breast. Thumb playing with the nipple.

Kacy leaned into him, arms around his shoulders. He kissed. She probed his mouth with her tongue.

And pulled away. Out of his reach.

A wicked, wicked smile graced her lips. She grabbed his shorts.

Unzipped, and pulled down both the cargo shorts and boxers.

His cock popped free. Aroused, but not fully erect yet.

Kacy wanted to change that.

She went down on her knees. His manhood was crowned by a close cropped patch of pubic hair.

Just the tip first. A taste. Josh throbbed between her lips.

Sliding down further, careful to not to scrape her teeth on him.

Down, down. Near the base. She breathed through her nose, eyes closed.

Kacy massaged his balls. Josh tasted wonderful. Far too long since she'd experienced a man like this.

He grabbed a fistful of her hair, tugging Kacy to her feet.

And then pushed her onto the bed.

Josh tore away her bikini bottom. The last shred of her modesty.

Kacy touched her clit. Her pussy was wet, dripping. She hadn't realized it.

She hadn't realized how much modesty had been tossed out the window to get this man into her bedroom.

Her legs were wide open for him. So were her arms.

The penetration was sweet and gentle. Her pussy stretched. And tightened around him.

Josh hit her G-spot. A flood of pent up frustration washed across her body.

The headboard rattled. The box spring squeaked. Josh kept pounding, lost in his own lust.

Words formed on her lips. Nonsense to her own ears.

Begging.

Pleading.

Kacy was helpless under him.

She wanted desperately for him to go faster. To blow his load inside her.

She wanted to pinch his nipples and make him turn onto his back.

So she could fuck him as hard as she pleased.

For now, this time, she reveled in the loss of control in her own bedroom. Her own private space where she commanded her orgasms with electric toys.

This time, tonight, his hot and sweat covered body pressed against hers.

Josh rocked her senseless. His rod pumped her wet pussy, making squishing noises.

Legs wrapped around him, Kacy bucked against his thrusts.

Faster.

Harder.

More violent.

Her moans loud. Josh grunted.

Kacy slowed her motions down. An orgasm overtook her.

A gushing.

Painful, exquisite release. Starting in her pussy, ending in her toes and fingers. Kacy's entire body glowed. She dug her nails into his skin.

But Josh pumped faster against her. She was near numb, and exploding with sensations.

Hot. Cold. Wet pussy. Dry mouth.

He pulled out of her. His face scrunched, lost in his own orgasm. Josh's cock exploded. Hot, sticky cum slicked across her abdomen. She wondered if he would ever stop coming.

When he did, he fell on top of her, and made out with her. Josh fell asleep soon after, in her arms, and Kacy allowed herself to join him.

Her last thoughts before drifting off were fantasies of how she'd be on top next time.

When she woke, a dog barked downstairs, and the front door closed shut. A note was on the bed side table, scrawled in sloppy handwriting.

See you tomorrow night? -J.

He left his phone number as well.

The day was going to be far too long.

Kacy hoped the next night would be even longer.

The Glowing Satisfaction of Pancakes

ONE

KYLE MIXED THE BATTER. The coffee maker chugged and gurgled, the dark roast aroma bringing a smile to his face as he made breakfast for two. Bacon sizzled on the griddle. A bowl of fresh strawberries, cantaloupe, and honey melon sat at the nook next to a whipped cream can.

Already nine in the morning. The sports news played on the TV in the background. He'd wasted enough time, reading and watching the news. The mornings of his days off were always the slowest.

Sleepy-head upstairs would be down soon enough.

Karen had kept him up late at night, in the hopes he'd sleep in like a "normal person." Bless her heart, she tried. He was a little tired, but completely and utterly wide awake.

He couldn't help it. He was a morning man.

Since they moved in together, they developed an understanding. He woke up at six whether he needed to go to work or not, and kept the noise down so she could sleep. She burned the midnight oil playing video games, with or without him.

Right above his head, something fell from the bed. The weak spot in the floorboards creaked under the pitter-patter of her feet. The toilet flushed. Her electric toothbrush vibrated.

Kyle set out two glasses of orange juice.

The feet clunked down the stairs. To be small boned and only five-four, Karen made a lot of noise.

He was washing dishes when she strolled into the kitchen. She greeted him with a hard smack on the ass.

"Good morning, sunshine," said Kyle.

"Yup," she said, throat raspy. Karen opened the fridge and stared inside. She wore her pink fluffy robe, tied just enough to reveal her flat bosom.

He didn't care for her padded bras, much preferring her teacup sized boobs the way they were. But she thought her bras made her look sexy, and Kyle was smart enough not to argue.

"Juice on the counter." He pointed to the nook.

"Ugh, huh," she said, slamming the fridge door shut. She shambled over to the nook and chugged her glass of juice. She sucked in a breath through her nostrils, stood in a tree pose, and slammed back his glass too.

"Coffee's about ready."

"Good."

He poured her a cup and mixed in cream the way she liked it.

Color flushed to her cheeks when she brought the cup to her lips and drank. Karen's face glowed. For her, caffeine was an aphrodisiac.

More precisely, a means to squeezing in more sex after work and after the sun went down. She had to work off the excess energy from video games somehow, or so she told him often enough.

"How do you do it?" Karen said.

"Say what?" he said, hiding behind his own mug.

"I fuck you three ways silly last night. And yet you're up at the ass-crack of dawn. How do I defeat you?"

Kyle shrugged. "Precision and grace?" The first reference to one of her favorite games, that he could think of.

"Fuck you!" Karen threw a kitchen rag at him. Square in the face. He caught it one handed, but only after it fell past his hips.

"Glad you're in a good mood this morning," he said.

"And if I was in a bad mood?" she said.

"Run for shelter?" He turned his back to her and poured batter on the griddle.

"Oh, I'd find you."

The sunlight now came in through the window, entirely too bright. A crisp stream of light that made a rainbow in his kitchen sink. He closed the blinds. The room darkened only slightly. But at least the sun couldn't peep in.

"You already done with your first?" he said.

"Yes, please." She pushed her coffee cup towards him. Half gone. He freshened it anyway, taking the opportunity to glance down at her half open robe. Karen thanked him profusely and took a careful sip.

Kyle flipped the pancakes. "Any plans? You know. Day off and all."

"Oh, I have plans," Karen twiddled her fingers together like a cute mad genius.

"And you'll let me know?"

"Soon as my belly is full."

A minute later, Kyle handed her a short stack with two crispy pieces of bacon. Karen dabbed a smidgen of butter on the top pancake, and then flooded the plate with syrup. Then she piled a handful of fresh fruit and whipped cream on top of everything.

Kyle sat down next to her with his own plate of bacon and pancakes.

"More joe, please." She placed her cup next to his. The coffee pot sat within arm's reach of both of them.

"I think you need to slow down, short-round," Kyle said.

"I'll flash a boob if you pour me coffee."

"We have a deal!"

He poured coffee, one eye on what he was doing, one eye on what she was doing. As best he could, at any rate.

Spilled not a drop.

Karen pulled back one side of her pink robe. Just enough for Kyle to spot the pink nipple crowning the tiny mound. He reached out to cop a feel. The fuzzy robe tickled the end of fingers...

She slapped his hand away.

"I said nothing about touching," she said.

"I was sure you did," said Kyle.

"Nope."

"What's it cost to touch?"

Karen shoved a bite full of pancake into her mouth and chewed slow. She made the appearance of think-ing—thumb under chin, eyes pointed up, cute dimples in her cheeks.

He was certain she'd never answer.

"Look, buddy," she said at last. Karen drank some coffee. "I worked damn hard last night. All for naught, apparently. You can let a girl eat."

"What do you want to eat?" Kyle said, lifting an eyebrow and winking.

"Pancakes." Karen back-hand slapped him and turned away. "Seriously, I'm hungry."

"Me too."

"Good."

"Yes."

"So, shut up already."

Kyle and Karen ate, mostly in wicked silence. He glanced at her, she at him. They washed away the taste of syrup with cantaloupe.

He fed her one last piece of fruit. And then he picked up her plate.

"Leave it," said Karen. She stood, loosening the robe. "Come into the living room."

"Why?"

"I'll show the cost of touching." Karen picked up the can of whipped cream.

TWO

KYLE GOT TOWELS FROM THE UPSTAIRS BATHROOM and hurried back down. His girlfriend was spread out on the couch, hands behind her head, feet crossed. The whipped cream sat on the coffee table.

The drapes were drawn shut tight. Scented candles burned over the mantelpiece. One might've been hickory. The other was almost certainly the lavender one he bought for her birthday. He never could be certain of scents.

Karen wiggled her toes at him.

He stood in the doorway, towels under one arm, erection already popping up. How could he be in the mood after last night?

"What's the price?" he said. "For touching."

"You'll see," said Karen. She didn't move. The image of pure laziness. Well deserved, he might add.

"You don't even know, don't you?"

"I like to make this up as I go."

"So I've noticed lately."

"You don't approve?" She sat upright, as if doing a sit-up. The robe slipped, revealing her creamy skin. Her tone was serious, high pitched a bit. He had no idea if she were teasing him.

"If I didn't?"

Karen smirked, and lifted her chin. "You like it. Say it."

"I like it very much."

"Say my name."

"Now you're being silly."

She pulled the robe tight across her bosom and crossed her arms. The pout on her face was to die for. Innocent and wicked at the same time.

"Karen."

"You give up too easy."

"Guess I'm easy like that."

Karen crossed her legs under her. Indian style, like they used to call in school.

Kyle tossed the towels on the edge of the sofa. He remained standing, hands crossed in front of him.

"Well don't be," she said. "I'll get bored."

"Don't want that." He wanted to follow up with some snarky response. Nothing came to mind, so he remained silent. And waited for Karen to take the lead. Something she excelled at. "Tell, what's the price?"

"Now you're jumping ahead of yourself," said Karen. "You have another price to pay entirely."

"What's that?"

"I'm cold." She shrugged her shoulders high and hugged herself. The room temperature was perfectly fine. Kyle was a little warm, if anything.

He suspected the warmth had nothing to do with the heat kicking in or the air conditioner not working. His erection had gone down, back to normal. From the glance downward, he guessed Karen had noticed.

She made him warm. The way she looked at him. The posture she was in, like a princess waiting to be waited on. The damned candles got to his head, making him feel woozy.

No. Not woozy. This was different, and he'd experienced it plenty of times around Karen. Now they'd been together for a year, and lived in the same house for the last month.

His girlfriend had an uncanny way of making him feel small. Despite her short stature and wiry frame. She had a strong chin and a big nose. Patrician. People who didn't know her, assumed she was arrogant. Or stuck up.

Kyle knew better.

She volunteered at the animal shelter. Wanted to adopt cats, but patiently waited for the "right one" to need a home. She generously loaned money to friends, and never expected to paid back. She was shrewd at business, and gave to charity.

"What are you staring at?" Karen said.

Kyle got down on his knees. He took both her hands in his. Her finger bones were so small and delicate compared to his rough hands. The nails were painted bright red, the skin satin smooth except for the left fingertips, the guitar calluses.

He kissed her knuckles.

"That's a start," she said.

"How much debt do I have to go?"

"Don't think about that. Think about what you're going to do to me."

"With pleasure. Might have to stop thinking though."

"What do you mean?"

"Too much thinking, I'll stop doing."

He kissed her wrist. The fuzzy robe tickled his nose. He sneezed, turning his head away just in time.

"That was sexy," he said. He pushed the sleeve up her arm.

"But can you recover?" she said, false mockery in her voice.

"You have doubts?"

Karen responded with a half grin, and tilted her head to one side.

He placed his hands on her knees and parted the robe just slightly. She wore nothing underneath, naked. Her privates were prickly with hair. She had shaved down there as an experiment, and now it was growing back. Kyle didn't let her shave him.

Karen had been disappointed, but didn't take it as a rejection. They had worked on their relationship in small steps, earning trust little by little.

Wow, had it payed off.

Kyle kissed her ankle. Another, lower. Still lower. Over the tan lines on her feet, where her strappy sandals covered. He knew what was coming.

She bucked and kicked her foot away.

"Hey!" she said, squirming. "That's not part of the price."

"Give me some direction."

Karen nodded. The wicked grin played across her face again. "Go north, young man."

He kissed her ankle again, and avoided touching her foot. Little, soft kisses up. One hand on the back of her calf, the other stroking around the kneecap. He did the same with the other leg, going only to the knees.

Karen played with his hair the whole time. Stroking, pulling, grabbing a fistful of hair. She yanked his head, to focus his kisses where she wanted.

He massaged her leg muscles. Her waxed skin was smooth to the touch, luxurious. Easy on the fingers and lips. She still tasted like the wild sex party from last night.

Tasted like a mixture of her and him.

Then he pressed further north. Head between her legs now, alternating his kisses on her thighs. Until he focused on one leg, closer to the sweet spot. She quivered beneath him, fingers pulling apart the robe more. One of her fingers brushed her clit, just once, but not very long.

Kyle pulled away.

"No, no, no," Karen said. "You're not done yet."

"I know what the price is," he said, voice husky. Needy. "And we're both going to pay it."

He picked up the whipped cream can.

"Oh God," she said.

THREE

KAREN SPREAD HER LEGS APART. The robe split, revealing all of her bottom. Kyle pulled the sash. The rest of the robe fell apart lazily.

"So," said Karen, "what's my price, big boy?"

"The price," he said, spraying a dollop of cream on one of her nipples, "is to tease the hell out of you." Another dollop, on the other nipple.

"I like this." She pressed the cream with her middle fingers, and licked one, then the other.

Kyle pressed his lips against her belly button, kissing. Karen squirmed under his touch, sucking in her stomach. Laughter, clear and happy, erupted from her. He shook the can and sprayed cream on her navel.

"Don't I taste good enough?" she said.

"Well, we could both use a shower," he said.

Karen smacked him on the side of the head and laughed some more. Yes, a shower. This was going to be a long day. Why did he have to wake up so early?

He kissed the cream. It stuck to his lips like a weird, foamy goatee. The mouth prints he left leading down to her pussy were wet and hardly looked like a proper mouth. Too saggy and droopy, like bad finger painting.

"Give me the cream," said Karen.

"No."

"What do you mean? Don't you trust me?"

Kyle chuckled in response. He shook the can, and sprayed lower. A white, puffy line straight down from her navel to clit. And sprayed more, this time concentric circles on top of her pussy lips.

He pressed his face into her. The honeypot smelled like a combination of sweet sugar and wet girl fluids. He flicked his tongue across the surface.

And then dug deeper. Into the whipped cream, on her flesh. Hands on her hips now, he pressed inside her, licking her inside and out. His erection returned, at full attention. Kyle was vaguely aware when she took the whipped cream can from his hand.

He didn't fight her for it. Too distracted anyway.

Karen moaned. A wild, erotic sound loud enough to wake up neighbors. She ran her fingers through his hair. Gentle at first. The harder he licked, sucked, and fingered her, the more she tugged his hair. Her legs wrapped tighter, clutching him close.

Until she pulled his head away.

"Hey, I..." Kyle said.

Karen sprayed whipped into his mouth. Whatever was on his mind, was now lost.

"Shut up," she said. "Spread those towels on the couch."

Off came his shirt. He obeyed her command, with a satisfied smile. As he bent over to arrange the towels, she pulled down his pajamas and smacked his bare ass.

Karen got him to lay down on his back. She sat on the far of the couch, leaned forward, and sprayed whipped cream up and down his cock.

The sensation was cool and pleasant, like a moist and fluffy towel slapped onto his privates. She leaned forward and licked it all up, one lap at a time. Cream of both kinds slid down his shaft to his balls and down to his anus.

Karen licked off the last. But he had more to give. She sprayed a line of whipped cream up from his navel to throat. His erection throbbed, and he wanted to touch himself. Instead, he crossed his fingers under his head and waited patiently while Karen kissed and licked her way up his stomach.

He closed his eyes, and an eternity passed of sweet bliss. When she reached his throat, Karen grabbed his shaft and slipped him inside her.

Just the tip at first. Down, slow. She retreated. Through slitted eyes, Kyle enjoyed the torturous expressions on her face. He jabbed upwards, balls deep into Karen.

She grunted, and pressed her hips down harder on him. The pussy juice dripped down his balls now. Wet slapping sounds, skin on skin, became faster and desperate.

On top of the sugar, cock, and pussy smells; now the living room smelled of sweat. Kyle's body heated up as if from a fever. He fondled her breasts. The nipples were swollen and erect, and too hot to touch.

Faster she pumped.

Up. Down. Up.

He met her action with his own thrusts. Soon, they got into a see-saw rhythm with each other.

Karen pressed her palms into his chest, slowing the pace, easing up on cock. She gyrated her hips, yanking him to and fro. A devious smile curled her lips.

The pressure on his cock and balls built, throbbing.The excruciating pleasure was almost too much, and every bit as fun as last night.

Kyle grabbed her waist, stopping her motions. He sat upright, shooing her off of him. Turning her around roughly, he tore the fluffy pink robe from her body and tossed it aside.

He grabbed her hair and pushed her onto the couch, on her knees and hands. Karen reached around and grabbed his junk, pulling him toward her.

Entering from behind Karen, this time on his terms. Kyle pinned her to the couch, and slammed into her pussy.

Edging her. Teasing with the head. Quick pumps followed by slow, deliberate thrusts. Kyle lost all track of time. His entire body became hot. Karen moaned and whined nonsense, head down.

Kyle couldn't take the head anymore. His need became wild. Grabbing her ass in both hands, he fucked Karen harder.

She tossed her hair back, looking at him from over her shoulder. Eyes slitted. Breathe ragged.

Her pussy tightened on him. Hot juice poured out.

Kyle blew his load deep inside her.

And kept fucking. Easing off, a little at a time. Her pussy relaxed and tightened again.

He slipped out of her. His head felt light. Woozy.

Karen laid down on her back, arms behind her head. She blew him a kiss.

Kyle lay down on top of her, head on one flat breast. He closed his eyes, breathing already turning to snoring. She wrapped her arms and legs around him, like a warm cocoon.

So that was the price? Pancakes... and a mid-morning nap on her breasts.

After Hours on the Full Moon

ONE

H E SAT AT THE FAR END OF THE BAR, near the front doors and far away from the stage, facing away from Cheryl. A handsome man, but not like the regulars at all. Clean shaved, dark, roguish good looks but not Hollywood stunning. He wore jeans and a black dress shirt with the sleeves rolled up.

She watched him in the mirror behind the bar. Seemed like the nice type of man, with a nice smelling musky cologne that she thankfully couldn't smell from this far away and easy dimples in his cheeks. Not the type to be chasing a girl with tattoos on both arms.

Waiting for a date? Probably... He sat tall, back straight, shoulders relaxed.

Tonight the bar was hot. Uncomfortably so. Cheryl's panties felt wadded up in her ass crack, but maybe only because she was working so hard. She had bitched to Robert to fix the air or she'd leave for good this time. Bound to happen one day, anyway. Problem was, she enjoyed her night job, and the rent on the upstairs apartment was just right for a student.

Cheryl went up to the man, and wiped away peanuts and spilled beer from the previous customer. Squatter's Dive smelled constantly of spilled beer, peanuts, and fried cheese. Even on Saturday mornings when Cheryl came in to mop the floor, the smell was ever present.

The music was usually good, though tonight the guitarist and singer were out of key with each other. The cheese was always great.

"What's your poison?" She leaned forward, elbows on the bar, letting her low-cut tank top fall open a tad. Cheryl wasn't well endowed, but the men tipped well when she flashed a little skin.

He turned around in the barstool and flashed her a smile. His teeth were pearly white, and damned if he didn't have a twinkle in his eyes. Perhaps it was the funky blue and green lighting in the bar.

"Bacardi and Coke," he said. He glanced down at her breasts, and then looked her in the face. "No ice, please."

For once, Cheryl was disappointed a man stared into her eyes instead of lower.

"Sure thing, sweetie." She tossed a paper coaster in front of him.

He turned away, gazing again at the front doors. Like many of the guys who drank here, he'd probably leave with a girl on his arm.

Cheryl would have her law books, and she'd sleep naked with a battery operated toy.

The band hit the final chords of the song they were on and let the reverb hang too long. The drummer crashed the cymbals as if he wanted to purposely annoy every dog in a five block radius.

Usually the music was good. Tonight, Robert had hired a doozy of a band. They were retro-grunge with out of season flannel shirts and acid-eaten jeans. Cheryl couldn't even remember their name.

She made the drink and brought it to him. When the "music" died down enough for normal sound, she leaned forward again.

"Cheers, mate," she said.

He glanced back over his shoulder and grabbed the glass, hand just a hair away from her left boob. His mouth moved in what appeared to be a "thank you", but the band had already started up again. Sounded like "Kick Start My Heart", but without any discernible bass or recognizable lyrics.

Cheryl served, chatted, and flirted with her other customers. Old guys with receding hairlines and beer-bellies, handsome punks with pretty dates, ladies on girl's night out.

The man with the twinkle in his eye sat alone, but gave up his vigil on the front door, drink still not downed. He stared at Cheryl, and when she stared back with a wink and a smile, he found his rum and soda more interesting.

A drunk at table five threw a beer bottle at the stage, and hit the lead singer below the belt. The bottle left a liquid trail from his crotch down the torn up jeans to his fire-engine red Chuck Taylors, and shattered on stage.

The singer yelped and jumped back. The guitarist kept smashing the fretboard, face hidden by massive dreadlocks.

Bob the bouncer (not to be confused with Robert the manager) picked up the guy at table five by the scruff of the neck. The drunkard flailed his arms all the way to the door, smacking other patrons in the head on the way past.

Meanwhile, the singer knocked over his microphone, kicked the bass drum hard, and stormed off stage to the back room.

The dreadlock guitar boy caught a clue, stopped played mid-measure, and looked confusedly to his band-mates. They all walked off stage.

The entire bar applauded and cheered.

Cheryl used the humorous situation as a mask to keep smiling and nodding. She made her way back to the other end of the bar.

"Does this happen often?" said the roguish man in the black shirt.

"Only on Saturdays," said Cheryl. "Must be the full moon."

"I should come here more often."

"Waiting for a lady friend?" Cheryl couldn't help herself. She half hoped the lady was a tramp. Or didn't show up at all.

There really was a twinkle. His eyes were dark, Mediterranean. Italian descent?

"Yeah." Another good look at his pearly whites. "She recommends this place. Said she comes here all the time."

"Oh?" said Cheryl. "I work here all the time, seems. Maybe I know her."

"Perky. Blond. About my height."

"You described half the women here."

"At least I didn't describe you." He lifted his glass in salute, then, when thinking about his phrasing, meekly retreated the toast with slumped shoulders.

Cheryl smacked his wrist like a school teacher disciplining a youngster, leaning forward on the bar again, this time on only one elbow. She had dyed black hair, originally mousy brown, and sure in hell wasn't perky in the way he meant. About the right height though, or so she guessed. Hard to tell from the wrong side of a bar.

"What are you gawking at anyway?" she said.

"Oh. Nothing." He sipped his rum and Coke.

She poked his elbow. "Come on. I won't tell your girlfriend."

"Just admiring your tattoos."

Cheryl had a pair of twin dragons, one on each arm. Their tails wrapped around each other at her shoulder blades. The lithe bodies slithered in spirals down her arms.

"Check it out." She pressed her forearms together. The dragons' tongues kissed at top of her wrists.

"Wow," he said. "I... I've never seen that before."

"Hope you never do again," said Cheryl, winking. "Makes a great conversation starter here. Means I have to wear long sleeves at court."

"You at court often?"

"Only when I'm bad."

"What? I took you to be the warm cuddly type. My mistake."

"Fine, mister," Cheryl laughed. "But you only get one!"

A woman came in the door right then. Tall, blond, perky. With a Gucci bag and a cell phone pressed to her ear.

"Date's here," Cheryl pointed.

He turned around. Whatever slouch was in his shoulders disappeared. Color flushed in his cheek and ear. Cheryl found that cute.

The blond bitch couldn't be good enough for him.

"Not her," he said.

She was glad. For him, of course.

"She'll show up," Cheryl said. "Flag me down when you want a another, okay?"

She didn't intend a double meaning there.

He nodded anyway, the dimples returning.

She attended her other customers. Canned music now played from the speakers. Cheryl refilled his rum and soda. Then got him a Killian's. And a Rolling Rock.

More people flooded the bar, then left. Until after midnight the bar was near empty, odd for a Friday but no bother. The music was a quiet background beat. Bob mopped the floor. The line cooks punched out. Cheryl did her share of cleaning, and put on a fresh pot of coffee.

The full body bean aroma clashed and mixed with the smell of bleach and cleaning suds.

The man in the black shirt remained, alone on the same damn stool at the end of the bar, slouching over his beer bottle as if it were his only friend in the world. No perky blond hung on his arm.

The twinkle most certainly wasn't there.

T W O

CHERYL SET TWO CERAMIC MUGS in front of the mystery man who got stood-up, and poured coffee. Steam rose, perking her up after a long afternoon and night of work. Her feet were sore as hell inside her tennis shoes, the ache throbbing it's way up her calves and thighs.

Only the stragglers stayed behind, and they weren't hard to take care of.

"Coffee's on me," she said.

"Thanks," he said. "Looks like I need it?"

The reek of rum and beer overshadowed the nice cologne he'd come in with. His speech was slurred and slow. One of a bartender's superpowers is translating drunk talk. Sometimes that meant smiling and nodding at the right moments.

She didn't want to just smile and nod for him. No, this man deserved so much more, and maybe she could at least keep him company.

"Looks like you lost a fist fight to a kitten," said Cheryl, extending her red polished nails into a claw. "I could add some scratch marks to make it more convincing."

He laughed. Might've been the booze doing the work for him, but it sounded genuine from the pit of his stomach.

"Pete," he said.

Cheryl introduced herself. Pete grabbed her hand and shook it, squeezing her knuckle bones ever so slightly. He held on a long moment too much, eyes tracing the dragon's curved body up her wrist and forearm, to her bare shoulder.

"I'm sorry she didn't show," said Cheryl. She meant it too. Nobody deserved to go home lonely. Especially a man like Pete.

Pete sipped his coffee. "Wow, that's hot!"

"The better to sober you," she said.

"Isn't your job to get people drunk?"

"It's a complicated affair." She brought the coffee to her nose, sniffed it. Smelled bitter enough to slay any bad mood, strong enough to resurrect the dead. "Need cream or sugar?"

"Both, please," said Pete. He sipped, and his face scrunched. He raised an eyebrow in mock astonishment. "Wondering if you were killing me with whatever this is."

Cheryl turned around to grab the creamer and sugar bowls. In the mirror behind the bar, she could see Pete. Watching her. Her jeans hugged her hips like a second skin, exactly why she wore them when working.

She was used to men staring, occasionally touching and being too forward. Part of the job, and she had ways to discourage without being off-putting. The attention was sometimes annoying, infuriating when from the wrong men, and—amazingly—at the same time empowering.

She stalled, letting Pete stare. Allowing him to imprint the image in his head.

"So," she said, spoiling his view by turning around. She set the cream and sugar by his cup. "Tell me about her."

"What? Oh," he said. "Nothing you want to hear."

"Pete," said Cheryl, and handed him the stir straws. "I'm a bartender. What else do you think I do? Besides get you drunk and then sober you with radioactive coffee?"

He chuckled, shaking his head, picking an orange colored straw and stabbed it into his coffee. Pete dumped two creams and three sugars, and stirred.

"I cleaned the entire house," he said at last. "Vacuumed the floors. Cleaned the bathtub and toilet. Washed a load of towels. Had fresh food on hand for breakfast."

"That's a lot of work for a no-show," said Cheryl.

Pete waved his hand, nodding sagely. He blew the steam off his coffee and took a another tentative sip. No scrunch or evil eye glare.

She leaned forward, on her elbows, not directly in front of him this time. She wasn't working for a tip anymore. The money was good tonight, near five hundred in cash. And he was nearly the last customer. A sacred bond existed between bartender and the final straggler to leave. It was the one-on-one attention with a stranger, the desire to notice and be noticed, and be the only two people in the universe for a moment.

He still glanced over at her breasts.

This time, the attention was empowering.

"We met at a birthday party," said Pete. "Mutual friend. Buddy of mine, in fact."

"Not a bad place to meet."

"Except when that band is playing," he pointed to the stage. "Last time the lead singer dumped a kegger on his head and fell on top of the crowd. The mosh pit let him fall on his ass."

"Too funny."

"Can't think of the band's name," he said.

"Me neither."

Damn the two word responses! What was wrong with her tonight?

They sipped coffee, the silence hung in the air between them like an Arabian java bean cloud. Cheryl stretched her legs out, one by one, the hamstrings and calves burning. Even though she couldn't wait to feel the cool touch of lube on her clit, Cheryl didn't want to go upstairs to her electric vibrator just yet. The night was too early, and Pete was too sexy. She'd never study tonight, even if she had to take the bar tomorrow at eight sharp.

How did she talk to complete strangers all night, but couldn't carry on a conversation with a handsome fellow?

"What was her name?" Cheryl asked. Stupid question! Why did she even care? Well, she was a bartender...

"Who cares?" said Pete. "I won't see her again."

"Why not? Maybe she had a good reason?"

"Cheryl," Pete leaned forward, lowering his voice as if to share a secret. Without thinking, she leaned forward too, ear near his lips. "We were meeting for one reason."

"Oh?" she said, whispering in his ear. "Can I guess the reason?"

"I'll give you three. Bet you only need one."

"Hmm," she said. "I think you were going to watch movies with her."

Her voice came across sultry, as if she were having phone sex with Pete instead of chatting with him across from a bar. Cheryl shifted her hips. A small collection of porno movies were hidden inside her DVD cabinet. She'd had a long enough day, perhaps she was just telling him what she wanted to do.

"Kind of right," said Pete. Now his voice was husky and raw. His lips were so close to her skin, the fine hairs on her neck tingled. "Good thing I didn't really bet."

"Maybe you were going to play a game with her," said Cheryl. Sure, why not tell him what she wanted? No one ever got hurt with a little harmless flirting. Especially when it wasn't direct.

"You could say that," he said.

This close, Pete's cologne smelled so musky and warm, only slightly overshadowed by alcohol and joe. Cheryl stuck her ass out further, imagining what it'd be like if he were behind the bar with her, fucking her doggy style.

She touched his arm with the tips of her fingers. His skin was hot, the coarse hair smooth to the touch. Closer, near enough to bite his ear. The tip of one breast so close, all he had to do was reach up and grab if he wanted.

Her lips moved, but her brain had little control now. "And then strip her down like a naughty whore and..."

"Whoa! Which of us is drunk? I forgot."

"I'm sorry," Cheryl said, bolting upright. Blood rushed to her head, flushing her cheeks hot. Her fingers wrapped around her mug's handle, and she brought the coffee to her lips to hide. "It's late. I've worked all day. Didn't have to go there..."

Pete held up hand and limp-wrist waved. "No worries. Unless you treat all customers like this."

"No."

"Too bad. I was thinking of recommending all my buddies come here."

"I can only make one man come a night. One of my rules."

Pete reached into his back pocket and got out a brown, stained and beaten up wallet. "I'd like to know some of your other rules."

"What for?" said Cheryl.

"So I can play your game," said Pete. "What do I owe?"

"On me. Phrasing... The drinks are on me, cowboy."

He laughed, color spreading across his cheeks and down his neck. His smile was infectious and disarming. Cheryl couldn't help but share in the humor.

"I must owe something," Pete said. He pulled out a hundred dollar bill. "Just feels wrong otherwise."

"What kind of woman do you take me for?"

"The kind I'd take home to mother."

"Aw, how sweet." Cheryl lightly smacked his cheek with her fingertips. "But before that happens, my apartment is upstairs."

A tense, silent moment passed. Pete folded the Ben Franklin in half, gaze downward as if pondering life's mysteries. Cheryl held her breath, wondering what would happen next. Would he respond to her come-on in good humor, and they'd laugh it off like good friends?

Did she need her toy tonight?

Pete reached out, and shoved the money down her low-cut tank top, inside her bra just above the lace. Her heart hammered against the touch, his fingers warm and rough.

"I finish here in an hour," Cheryl said.

"Can't wait," he said. "Gives me enough time to sober up."

"I'd appreciate that," she took his hand and leaned forward as if to kiss him. "One more thing."

"Anything."

"What's her name?"

"Really? Why?"

"Just tell me."

"Brenda," he said.

"I promise one thing," said Cheryl. "By the end of the night, you won't remember her name."

THREE

THE NEXT HOUR PASSED UNEVENTFULLY, but tense. Cheryl cleaned, taking breaks only to stretch her aching back and legs now and then. A hot shower would hit the spot, but she couldn't help but think about the spot she hoped Pete would hit.

He used the restroom twice, and drank two more cups of bitter sugar-filled coffee. He talked with Bob the bouncer, watched the late night talk show on the big screen TV, and relaxed in a way he hadn't earlier. Before the coffee, he'd been either slouching or sitting upright as if a pole had been shoved in his ass. Now he was poised, confident, shoulders thrown back, but at ease.

Cheryl tried hard not to stare at him. Staying busy helped. There was a floor to mop, glassware to get to the dishwasher, prep work for the next shift.

Then she'd take a sip from her now cold and stale coffee, and stare at Pete through the mirror. Watching him laugh at the TV, dump more sugar into his java, run his fingers through his thick hair.

And then she'd see Bob in the mirror too, shaking his bald head and chuckling. He worked fast, a skip to his step, taking out trash and wiping down tables as if giant red devil were lashing him to move ever quicker. Maybe he had someone waiting for him at home.

The whole time, Cheryl wondered: *Would Pete mind if I showered first? Could I get him into the shower with me? Do I want to do that? Should I shave my twat? Would he like that?*

The hour dragged on for an eternity of questions with no answers, and then it ended. The last drunkards left. Bob bid her a good night with a knowing wink. Cheryl tossed the coffee mugs on the dish-line for the morning crew.

"You ready?" she asked, keys in hand.

"What do you think I was doing in the bathroom?" Pete said.

"Draining the booze out of your system." She locked the front doors and punched in the code on the pad for the security system. "And that better be all you drained, mister."

He shrugged, hands in his front jeans pockets. "It's mostly gone."

Cheryl rolled her eyes and yanked one hand out of his pocket. His palm was warm and sweaty. She led him through the kitchen, past the ripe smells of burnt meat and fried food, up the back stairs with the creaky steps, unlocked her apartment door, and pushed him inside.

"Mi casa, su casa," she said, waving one arm gracefully about.

"Lovely place," he said. "Not what I expected above a bar."

"What you expected? Lava lamps and shaggy green carpet?"

When first moving in, that had been what the place looked like. Since, she'd blackmailed Robert into painting the walls and putting down a cream colored carpet, giving the old hangout a clean and fresh, homey smell.

Not an ounce of remorse passed her brain, since the apartment needed a remodel to match the downstairs renovations.

Cheryl kicked off her tennis shoes at the door, and Pete did the same. The main room was small and cozy, big enough for a three-person sofa, a TV, some tables, and a whole lot of books.

Pete pointed at the bookcases lining the wall adjacent to her thirty inch TV. "More like, I didn't expect a library of law textbooks."

"Oh, you know. Girl's got to have hobbies."

"So you're a law student?" he said.

"Cliche."

"But awesome." Pete's dark, Italian eyes lit up. "Guess you weren't joking about being in court."

"I'm second year. With luck, I won't need the bartending gig much longer."

"Good," he said. "I mean, for you. I did similar stuff when I was a student. Waiter, retail clerk, other things I don't want to mention."

"Oh?" Cheryl dropped her keys in the crystal ashtray, on the hickory hutch behind the sofa. "Anything I'll see you in court for?"

"Naw, nothing like that. Just didn't care for those jobs."

She yanked on his dress shirt, the silky smooth fabric slick under her fingers, and maneuvered him to the sofa. One leg folded up beneath her, she sat first. He followed suit, tilted away from her at an angle.

"What do you do now?" Cheryl didn't entirely let go of his shirt, his chest and ab muscles firm under her touch. Pete tensed when she wandered near his belt.

"I own Eighth Street Books," he said, clutching her hands in his. "Not far from your school."

"Really? Do you carry law books? Maybe I'll stop by sometime."

"Maybe I'd like that."

"Maybe?" Cheryl inched closer, still keeping a safe distance.

"Well, assuming you don't kill me tonight. Otherwise, yes."

"What if I kill you only a little bit?" Closer. Enough to sneak a peck on the lips if she chose. Far away enough to retreat if she creeped him out too much.

"La petit mort?" he said.

"*Oiou*," she said, eyes half shut, lips so very near his. Electricity fizzled between them.

Pete cupped a hand behind her head, bringing her the rest of the way.

He kissed her first.

A sweet, gentle peck, followed by the press of wet lips and his tongue. Blood rushing to her head, Cheryl shivered in the excitement. Every nerve raw and frayed, she loosened to the rhythm of his kissing.

It had been far too long since she'd last been touched like this.

Fumbling about with limb and body positions, she climbed onto Pete, into his lap, her legs straddling his waist. She pinned him to the couch. No escape for him now. Pete wrapped his arms around her torso, bringing her into his warmth, like a cocoon.

Lips locked, fingers shaking, Cheryl teased the buttons of his shirt, not quite getting two undone. The skin underneath was smooth like polished glass and burnt fiery hot. Shaking with frustration, Cheryl pushed herself away. She hadn't noticed she stopped breathing. Each pant hurt like a rough tickle.

"This," she said. "This is your last chance. To escape."

Pete grabbed her forearms, sliding his hands up the dragons' bodies.

"Which way to the bedroom?" he said.

FOUR

CHERYL DRAGGED PETE INTO HER BEDROOM, unbuttoning his shirt along the way, as best she could at any rate. She hit the light-switch with her elbow and yanked off her top.

The room was just big enough for a queen size bed and a night table. It smelled clean, the floor had been vacuumed not long ago, and she'd made the bed this morning. Not bad for an unplanned one-nighter.

She pulled back the bed covers.

The curtains were still open. She went to the window, fingers on the drawstring to close the blinds. Outside, the full moon shone bright.

Pete touched her shoulder blades, tracing the curved lines of dragon tails to her arms. He pushed her hair out of the way, and kissed her neck, right below the ear. A tingly, raw sensation settled into the pit of her stomach and spread out across her body, into her limbs.

Stranger things happened on full moon nights.

Cheryl dropped the blinds and closed the curtains. Half turning, she wrapped her arms around his neck and pulled his dress shirt down his shoulders. Pete pulled her in, kissing her, exploring her mouth with his tongue.

A belt buckle loosened and rattled. Cheryl dug her fingernails into his hair, yanking and pulling his head about to kiss him deeper. A zipper unzipped. Pants dropped to the floor. Silky boxers rubbed against her bare stomach.

Pete was already hard. The tip was wet.

He pushed her to the bed. Cheryl gasped for breath, undoing her own belt buckle. Eager, sweating, fingers not entirely functioning right. Pete helped her with the zipper and yanked off the tight jeans one leg at a time. The black lace panties slid off too.

She reached out and pulled down his boxers. His cock flopped out, springing at attention. Pete was just the right size, above average, a big mushroom head, a tight ball sack.

Cheryl clung to him, legs wrapped around his. Sucking and licking his nipples, she stroked him one handed, gliding gently up and down his shaft. She stroked the tip, feeling the ridges and the hot, sticky precum pouring out of him. Pete shivered and gasped and pulled her hair.

The room heated up. Boiling hot. Fingers pressed into her shoulders. Pete pushed her onto her back. He placed a pillow under her head, and adjusted his body over hers. She spread her legs, letting him kiss her, hoping for more.

One finger on her clit, Pete rocked her steady. Her body tightened, heart pumping fast, every part of her numb and sensitive at the same time.

Her pussy became wet. He massaged her faster, dipping a finger inside, pulling out. She wanted to stroke him. Get his cock inside her. Something... but she was trapped underneath him, at his mercy.

Finally, slow and gentle, Pete slid deep into her, stretching her out little by little. Cheryl gasped when he was balls deep. She clung to him by the neck, wrapping her legs around his waist. A sweet moment of sweaty bliss passed, face to face, lips touching but not locked, bodies pressed together in a hot mess.

Cheryl bucked against him, wanting more, now. His breath was sultry hot. Still, quiet, moving only a nudge, Pete rotated his hips. She closed her eyes to slits. Every nerve in her body screamed for attention.

One more kiss, sweet and wet. And then Pete pumped. Again and again, faster. Rougher with each thrust.

He slowed, catching his breath, letting her catch hers, and shared a kiss. Pete took her hand, his fingers entwined with hers, and he pinned her to the bed with his other hand in her hair. The bed squeaked and moaned under their bouncing. She breathed in short gasps, her heart pounding faster and faster.

Time blurred and slowed for Cheryl. Their skin made thwapping noises. Louder, harder. Closer.

Her pussy tightened and spasmed around his cock. She shuddered against his body, her orgasm rattling her to the core.

Pete pulled out inch by excruciating inch. Still holding her hand, he stroked himself. Face tensed, brows pinched together, he squeezed her hand tighter. A hot spurt erupted across her stomach, across her bra. Some of it sprayed on her chin. He sighed, relaxing back into her embrace, pressing his semen between them.

Another kiss, this time lazier, half-hearted with no tongue. Pete flopped over on his side, opening his arms, welcoming her to sleep.

She laid side by side with him, warm fluids from both of them coating her body. Settling into his arms, something crinkled underneath her, near her breast.

Cheryl slipped two fingers into her bra, and pulled out the hundred dollar bill Pete had tipped her. Chuckling from exhaustion, she flicked the money away and closed her eyes.

The Girl Behind
the Counter

J ASON HAD GONE TO THE QUICKIE MART gas station every Thursday through Saturday night on
his way to the job at the cinema. It was cheaper to
buy a sandwich and soda at the station than at work,
even with the employee discount on concessions. Then
every night on his way home around three in the morning he'd drive back and stop again for some late night
munchies.

Only rarely did the redhead chick get a night off.
Jason at first was nice to her, always in a hurry to get
to work. After a few months of that job, he learned he
could afford to be a few minutes late. So he'd be nice
and chat with the girl for awhile, since it seemed like

she was often bored and lonely at the gas station. She had a nice handful sized rack, pretty skin, and an ass to die for. Her name tag announced her as Miranda, he noticed one day while taking a quick glance at her perky breasts.

"So," he said, "Miranda."

"Yes?" She checked out his box of candy and soda and tapped her nails while he slid his card.

"Hi."

"Hey you." Her smile was to die for. He wondered what her smile would look like in the low lights of his bedroom when he got home from work. "You want something?"

"No, I'm good. Just wanted to say have a nice day."

"Have a good night." She smiled again, this time forced and coldly professional.

Jason cursed himself out on the way to work, nearly tail ended a woman, and ran through a red light. He'd screwed that up, and couldn't have gotten any worse. *What a dumb ass*, he kept thinking and telling himself over and over. Pretty young girl all alone and being friendly to him. And he didn't have the balls to ask her on a date?

He went through the motions at work, taking movie tickets, checking out pretty girls with dates, smiling at children. He made short work of the late night clean up and punched out before his boss could ask him to stay late. She was always on him to stay later, to help her clean up or something. He didn't want to fulfill her fantasy of having him in the theater after hours. Not like he wouldn't do her, but he was already pissed at himself for screwing up with the cutie at the Quickie Mart.

Back at the gas station, he picked up a few groceries. Miranda stood behind the counter, looking bored and tired. "Jason, buddy."

"Hey Miranda," he said. "How'd you know my name?"

"I'm psychic, of course," Her smile turned bright and cheerful, white teeth and pouty red lips. "I can see it on my screen when you swipe your card. Going to your next job?"

"Nope. Home for the night and I intend to sleep in for a few days. Why are you here so late?"

"No ride. Besides, I could use the extra hours."

"I hear you. Hope your ride shows up soon. Not exactly the kind of place I'd like to work at night."

"Fuck's sake, no. But my ride totally canceled on me at the last moment. The night auditor is here, but is taking a nap since I'm stuck with him."

Jason slid his card through the machine and hit credit. "Hey, I can give you a ride. If you want."

"Really?"

"Unless you want to stay here with the napping auditor?"

"I'll wake him up and get my shit."

"I'm parked out front here." Jason pointed to his Civic through the front window. "I'll wait up."

Miranda thanked him profusely, her smile getting bigger as she ran off to the back room. Jason packed his groceries in the trunk and sat listening to the radio for what seemed like forever. Snow fell, he adjusted the heat, turned the wipers on, turned up the defroster. He wondered if maybe this was a bad idea. And he kept reminding himself that he was just being a nice guy to a lady who needed some help. This wasn't a date, wasn't an invitation to sex. Just take her home.

And then go home and watch late night movies all night while eating frozen pizza. Sounded like a lovely night. Such a lovely night that he had been repeating every night for the last few years. He entertained the possibility of bringing Miranda back to his place, at least for a moment.

As soon as she walked out of the gas station with purse in hand, he threw that idea out the window.

Jason spared a glance at her profile—long red hair tied in the back, pale face in the sharp lime security lights, small nose with a piercing that seemed to shine in the dark. Miranda glanced up and down at him as she buckled her seatbelt, and he turned his focus to reversing the car and driving. No use admiring a pretty face while running over a garbage can. Maybe he could sneak a kiss on the cheek before she told him good night. He imagined the scene in his head a little to clearly—her eyes up at his, small hands on his torso as she leaned forward to accept the kiss...

He swerved to the right, an angry bystander flipped him off on the sidewalk. "Sorry. Long day I guess."

"Sorry to keep you up late."

"I'm a night owl normally." He leaned his elbow on the window and brooded. "Nope. Long work day, maybe. I was distracted."

Miranda laughed, a sweet curly laugh, deep and womanly, somewhat like a child giggling at a secret. "Distracted by what? The guy in the Packers shirt?"

Jason couldn't help but smile. He raised a palm up and shrugged. "You know me. I'm a sucker for anything Packers."

"Is that so? Well, you'll love my apartment."

"Let me guess," Jason raised a finger, "green wallpaper. Favre posters. Yellow carpet."

"So close. I prefer Doug Flutie as an idol. But I do have a Favre poster."

"I like you already. Did I mention that before?"

"You didn't." Miranda looked out the window, and hummed to herself. Nothing was said for a few minutes, Jason struggled to find more to say—he wasn't really much of a football fan, but he appreciated a girl who knew sports. *Why the hell didn't he ask her out yet?*

"You want to do something? Monday and Tuesday is my weekend."

"Maybe I have a boyfriend."

"I didn't say candle light dinner with wine." He scratched his nose, heart sunk to the bottom of stomach. Why were the pretty girls always taken? "I'd say a movie, but I work at a theater. Spend enough time there as it is."

She laughed again and slapped him on the arm. Her laugh was beginning to sound like a siren call—lovely and deadly, and something he needed to keep in perspective before he had a pissed off boyfriend with a shotgun chasing him down. "I'd say we could hang out at the gas station, but I spend a lot of time there."

"So no movie and no slushies from Quickie Mart. Gotcha. How about bowling?"

"I suck at anything with balls. I like mini golf though."

"So you only watch sports? I took you to be athletic."

"Track and swimming."

"Awesome. I used to do cross country, you know, back in the day."

"I don't miss those days."

"Who does? Hey, what street do I turn down?"

Miranda pointed down a number of streets. He drove in what seemed like circles and was close to lost in the weird neighborhood full of houses that all looked the same. Mostly split level and all of them with cheesy white fences out front. Garden gnomes watched him drive by as if taunting him.

"Right here," Miranda pointed. "The house without the fence."

"This cape cod thing? Gotcha."

He pulled in the driveway and put the car in park. He unlocked the doors while she gathered her purse.

"Thank you for the ride home," she said. "My roommate apparently decided to have a wild night at the clubs, even though I begged her to give me a ride home."

"Not a reliable friend? Sorry."

"I love her too much to move out. I just need regular rides."

"Doesn't everyone." Jason coughed. *Why the fuck did he say that?*

Miranda slapped him on the thigh. Her hand didn't leave his leg. "So you want to have coffee?"

"Do I get to meet you boyfriend?"

"I said *maybe* I have a boyfriend. So unless one just materializes out of nowhere, you probably won't get to meet him."

"I'm disappointed. So looking forward to meeting the chap."

"I bet you were."

"I could use a cup of coffee. But I need to bring my groceries inside so they don't spoil."

"My fridge is yours. Come on." She winked while unbuckling her seat belt. Jason tried to keep his emotions in check. It was just an honest coffee, and she was a stranger. No need to think it was more. It probably wasn't.

She had lied about the carpets, they were more of a faded beige than yellow. The wallpaper was a puce green, like somebody from the seventies had thrown up on the walls. He wondered if the Favre poster was in her bedroom, and if he'd get a chance to see it.

Miranda put on a pot of coffee while Jason pretended to read the front page of the newspaper. She was a hottie—cute tight rear end, nice curves all around, a sexy knockout smile—and those eyes killed him when she turned around from the kitchen sink. "I'll put on something more comfortable. Help yourself to the coffee mugs."

She opened the far cabinet where the mugs were on her way past. He thanked her, and couldn't help but notice how she swayed her hips when she walked. Jason thought he'd play this smooth, maybe get a good night kiss on the way out the door, and perhaps get a date lined up. That would make him the happiest man on the planet.

He pulled out a U of M mug and poured coffee for himself, and got a mug with a Dilbert cartoon out for her. He found creamer in the fridge. Miranda came back wearing tiny flannel shorts and a pink tank top.

He handed her the U of M cup. "Aw, thanks. How did you guess I liked it black?"

"Lucky guess I suppose." He poured coffee in to the Dilbert cup. "I like your choice of mugs. Did you go to the U of M?"

"Awhile back. Didn't finish. You know. School wasn't right for me at the time."

"That's too bad. Ever thought of going back?"

She gulped coffee and winced at how hot it was. "Now and then. No clue what I'd do though. I suppose I missed out on the college experience."

"Not really. If you went for a year, you had more than enough. I got a degree in accounting, hasn't gotten me a decent job in five years."

"I'm sorry to hear that," she squeezed his bicep. "Keep trying."

"Well, silly me for trying to be an accountant. I thought it'd be a safe career choice, but it ended up being too boring for me."

She took him by the hand and led him to the couch, and before things got too weird she turned on the TV. "I don't watch much. Anything you want to watch?"

"I only watch Craig Ferguson these days. I don't want to keep you up."

"You're not keeping me up."

Jason was up, but not in the sense of being awake. The coffee was strong and he was getting hard sitting next to Miranda. Her arm was pressed against his, her warmth seeping into his shirt. And she was looking at him, angled just enough so one boob tip touched him, full lips, eyes up cast at him. He kissed her on the lips once, no tongue.

Miranda set her mug on the table, and took his mug out of hand and set it beside hers. She pulled him by the shirt closer to her and kissed him, this time with tongue. His hands slid around her waist, feeling her lithe body up and down. Miranda pushed him back on the couch and sat on his lap, her legs wrapped around him.

This time, he pulled her closer, her hair between his fingers while he sank his tongue in her mouth. She pulled his hair and grinded her hips on him. His dick came full to attention while she moved all over. He slipped his fingers across one breast for a moment, then grabbed her thigh and hip, looking for the places that turned her on.

She pulled away, hands on his shoulders, panting. "Sorry. I... I didn't mean to."

"I'm having fun."

"Of course. You're a guy." She slapped him lightly on the chest. "You sure you want to do this?"

"I didn't bring a condom." Jason moved her off of him. "So probably not a good idea."

Miranda pouted, but the pout didn't last long when he smiled at her. She wrapped her arm in his and leaned against his chest. "Another time? Maybe?"

"I'd love to. Though, I have to say, I don't move this fast usually."

"Then why'd you kiss me?"

"Because your lips were there." He laughed. "Really. You have beautiful lips."

Miranda snapped her fingers and bolted upright. "My roommate!"

"Oh. If she'll be home soon I can leave."

"No," she gripped the front of his shirt in both hands. "She keeps extra condoms in her room."

Jason took her by the hand and pulled her up. "Let's do this."

"Let's fucking do this." Miranda lead him upstairs and told him to wait outside the first door. "She's a messy housekeeper. I'll be right out."

She shut door, cursed her roommate's name a few times, and came back out waving a condom between forefinger and thumb. "Ready big guy?"

"Need you ask?"

Miranda squinted, her brows pinched sharply as she tapped the condom against her lips. "Yes. I do."

"What if I said no?"

"I'd say good night, burn the voodoo doll I made for you, and come visit you in the hospital."

"Really? And you think I'd like you more if you played nurse for me?"

"Would you?" Only the slightest hint of a smirk peeped out of the corner of her mouth.

"Do you have a nurse's uniform?"

"Do I have a nurse's uniform? Do you mean the scrubs they wear in real hospitals?"

"Maybe."

"Hold on to this," Miranda tapped the condom package on his chest. He suppressed a smirk as he took it, the skin on his face heating up and blushing. She walked around him slowly, one breast touching his bicep. "You have some weird fantasies, Jason my man."

Jason pivoted as she brushed passed him, taking in her scent, wondering in his mind how this night was going to end. She opened the door behind him, motioned him to wait outside, and closed the door behind her. Pressing one ear up to the door, he heard the rustling of fabric and a closet door opening. Something heavy and made of cardboard fell, followed by an *ah shit*. If there was a time Jason wanted x-ray vision, it was now. His cock got stiff while he thought about Miranda in her underwear—assuming she was wearing any—scavenging in her bedroom closet for whatever outfit she had in mind. He would have done her in the skimpy shorts and tank she had been wearing. Or rather, after he took those garments off of her.

He leaned against the door frame, closed his eyes, and waited. Soon enough the door opened again, and Miranda stood a few feet away from him in a skin tight white nurse's costume with a red cross stitched to the left of one breast. The outfit was just long enough to conceal her panties. Her legs were covered in knee-high black leather boots.

"Sorry, baby."

"For what?" He looked her up and down, spending a long half second glancing at her squished up boobs.

"I disappointed you," Miranda placed one hand on her hip. "I know how much you like naughty girls in scrubs."

"You have no idea."

"You going to undress me with you eyes from the hallway," she beckoned him with a wink and a curled index finger, "or shall I send you a written invitation?"

"Do I need to RSVP?" Jason took one step and she grabbed him by the shirt collar, yanking him the rest of the way in. He had enough to time to notice the queen size bed, a pink alarm clock, and the Favre poster on the wall before she slammed the door shut and pressed him against the frame. Miranda pulled hard on his shirt sleeves, the seams popping enough he was certain he lost a few stitches, while she French kissed him.

Jason placed his hands on her hips, slowly massaging little circles in the white polyester costume, and played tongue tag with her. He'd nearly forgotten what a woman felt like, smelled like. Work, work, work... Very little time to play, or date for that matter. Miranda moaned softly, her hot breath coming in spurts.

He gripped her waist and pushed her away. Catching his breath, he threw the condom on the bed, and they shared a brief moment looking in one another's eyes. Hers were half closed, the pupils dilated in the low bedroom lights. She touched the corner of his lips, a wispy touch from the tips of her fingers. Jason took her hand and kissed the knuckles. Half a heartbeat later he grabbed her elbows, turned her around, and pressed her back against the door.

Shirt off, belt whipped off and thrown to the side, he smothered her with a fresh round of kisses. Miranda pulled a fistful of his hair as she flicked her tongue across his, and gyrated his head back as her kisses went lower down his neck to his chest. A shudder filled his body when she rolled her tongue across the nipple. Eyelashes fluttering, she looked up at him, laughed, and pushed him down on his knees.

He pulled her black lacy panties to the floor, letting his fingertips glide across her thighs, down and then back up to the hips. This time, he looked up at her and winked. The wet pussy smell overtook him as he buried his face between her legs. Soft moans and a tight grip on his hair encouraged him as he flicked his tongue across her clit. Middle finger probing her hole, he glanced up to watch her watching him—a big smile on her face, a hand stroking one breast, half-closed eyes, hair disheveled.

Miranda pushed him away from her pussy, her own finger pressing the clit, and squeezed her thighs together. A sultry moan escaped her teeth as he stroked her legs and knees. With some gentle massaging he coaxed her legs back open, wider, a little wider yet, the pink folds opening like flower petals, glistening wet in the dim bedroom light. She thrust her pelvis out and allowed him one last lick and suck before pushing his head away again.

She strutted to the bed, half-turned, beckoning him with open arms. Jason crawled on hands and knees to her, grasped the smooth leather boot calf on the way to sitting on the edge of the bed. She twisted his nipples and pushed him on to the bed, unzipped him and tore his pants off.

"Buddy," she purred, grasping his cock in one hand, using the fingernails of the other to scratch up and down his thigh. "My little buddy."

A shiver ran up his spine when she took him in her mouth, cold sweat broke out on his hot skin. Miranda teased his head with soft licks and husky moans, a gentle touch of lips, a tug on his balls. Arms behind his head, Jason closed his eyes and savored the sweet sucking noises she was making and all the sensations in his throbbing cock. Teeth scraped down his shaft, followed by a wet tongue and more moans.

"Stop," he could barely breathe. "Not now."

"What's wrong?" Miranda slapped her face with his cock. "Too much for you?"

"No. The problem is..."

He sat up on his elbows and gazed at her for a long moment. Miranda ran fingers through her hair. The light made her eyes all the more green and alluring.

"The problem is," he stood up and took her by the elbows, "you're still dressed."

Jason hugged her, kissed her neck, and unzipped the nurse outfit and let it slide off her. She unclasped her bra in a quick motion and threw it to the side. This time, he pinched her nipples, pushing her to the bed.

She lay on her back, arms wide open, legs spread apart. He ripped the condom package open and slipped the rubber on, barely containing his excitement. On top of her, he teased her pussy with the tip of his cock as he kissed her neck, slowly making his way down her chest, to an erect nipple. Miranda clutched his shoulders, breath shallow and fast.

"Oh God," she said, "fuck me. Fuck me, Jason."

Her pussy was moist and hot as he slid into her, both of them gasping. Slow, rhythmic pumping, in and out. Miranda seemed to lose control and turned to jelly beneath him, fingernails digging into his skin. A little faster, her moans were higher pitched and quicker.

Their sweaty bodies became one for a moment, electric sensations charging them both into a frenzy. Faster. Harder. Dirtier. The bed squeaked. She screamed his name. Her pussy clenched his cock and he exploded.

Jason rolled off her, catching his breath as he wrapped an arm around her and pulled the blankets over them. Miranda laid her head on his chest, panting, one finger toying with his nipple. Downstairs, the front door slammed and high heeled shoes clobbered their way upstairs.

"Sounds like your roommate is home," said Jason.

Miranda closed her eyes and grunted. Soon after, she snored.

Jason pulled in at the Quickie Mart like he always did before heading to work. The girl behind the counter winked.

"So," Miranda said, "Jason, buddy. Got any plans for tonight?"

He shrugged. "I've got a bottle of red wine chilling. Thought I'd pop that open after work."

"Drinking alone now days?"

"I have someone special to share with."

"Oh?" Her eyebrows pinched as she handed him his receipt.

"Thought I'd swing by her house. Invite her over. See what happens after."

"I'm sure she'd like that."

Jason smiled. The guy in line behind him coughed. Miranda smiled back. He shrugged again. "I'll see you later."

"I can't wait to find out what happens after."

"Me too," he whispered to himself.

DEAR READER,

Thank you for purchasing this book in trade paperback! Your support is amazing and appreciated. Because of you, I am fulfilling my career goals as a writer. With your support, I will continue creating fun stories that arouse and entertain folks like you all over the world. I enjoy what I do, and have a blast writing each story. I hope you enjoy reading them!

As a special thank you to those who bought the paper edition, I am offering a free e-book edition, so you can have this issue of Siren's Garter on your favorite device. Just use the coupon code **PL33E** at checkout on Smashwords (dot) com. If the code doesn't work, contact me directly at david (at) danthonybrown (dot) com, and I'll hook you up.

Again, thank you for being a reader!

Stay sexy,

David Anthony Brown
Content creator/publisher
Hermit Muse Publishing

ABOUT THE AUTHOR

Miriam F. Martin grew up wanting to be a cam girl, but excessive stage fright killed the dream. Her passion for getting strangers off over the wild worldwide web hasn't died yet. So she focuses her time writing smutty books for smart people, like you. When not writing erotica, she also writes science fiction and fantasy.

Her hobbies include playing the guitar badly, misinterpreting the future with Tarot cards, and over-analyzing dreams. She also enjoys first-person shooters, rogue-likes, and hidden object games. Her quest in life is to have a house full of cats.

Miriam loves to hear from her fans, and she may be contacted through her agent, David Anthony Brown, at:

david (at) danthonybrown (dot) com

ABOUT THE PUBLISHER

Hermit Muse Publishing is a sole-proprietorship located in the sunny hills of Minnesota, specializing in providing entertaining science fiction, fantasy, and erotica to readers worldwide. Hermit Muse is the home of D. Anthony Brown and Miriam F. Martin, both of whom are pseudonyms; and is the sole publisher of Siren's Garter, a bi-monthly erotica periodical.

www.ingramcontent.com/pod-product-compliance
Lightning Source LLC
Chambersburg PA
CBHW020605180626
46810CB00007B/2655